Invisible

Santita D'Anjou

ISBN: 978-0-578-82231-0 (Hardcover edition)
ISBN: 978-0-578-76041-4 (Softcover edition)
ISBN: 978-0-578-76042-1 (eBook edition)

For those of you who are struggling to find who you are. For the girl who doesn't feel pretty. For the boy who wants approval. For those of you who don't feel like you are enough.

You are not invisible.

Acknowledgements

To my dear friends, Tunisia Williams and Laila Avery, thank you for going on this journey with me. I so appreciate your time spent and advice.

To my husband, John, thank you for allowing me to be me. Thank you for sacrificing the time.

To my kids, John and Johanna, I love you both oh so much. Thank you for understanding when mommy needed quiet time.

1 | Too Little, Too Late

Legs burning. Sweating like I just ran a six-minute mile. I run up the stairs of the two-story holding pin. Clear View High. I'm late. Again.

Second period is almost over, so I don't bother going to class. I sign in at the office. The always-salty secretary, who never greets anyone, barely even looks at me. She rolls her eyes and hands me a bright green tardy slip. Why does she even bother to come to work? Every day she wears the same ugly attitude and jaded scrawl on her face?

"Have a GREAT day!", I shout.

She gives a satisfying jump and looks over her shoulder with a sharp stare. She shouts after me, "Jozi Skies, you better be on time the rest of this week!"

I ignore her. I smirk at the devious adrenaline running through me and head to third period.

The halls are peaceful without over two thousand students pressing up against each other, rushing to get to class. I lean against Kyell's locker to wait for the bell to ring.

My thoughts drift. Did Kyell realize I wasn't at school? I wonder if he's worried. Besides, he's the only person who seems to care whether I'm okay. My thoughts shift to my horrible parents. Would it really have held them up to peek in on me this morning?

A few moments later, the loud shrill of the bell jerks me back to reality. I glance in the direction of Kyell's classroom. Kyell, pronounced like sky-ell, but without the s. It's the kind of name that sticks with you. It's the one name you will remember out of a hundred people you just met.

My heart beats just a little faster as he turns the corner. I smile even though he hasn't noticed me yet. He paints vibrant color on the blank canvas of my world. He's the only reason I even come to this institution of marginalization. If it wasn't for him, I would be relaxing in my pajamas, completing eleventh grade from the comfort of my own home.

But he doesn't have a clue.

I doctor my hair a little bit, just to be sure it's not in disarray from the chaos of getting here. I run my hands up both sides of my bun, ensuring no stray curls have escaped. I quickly pull the sleeves to my hoodie down flinching at the tinge of pain running down my forearm. In all of the hustle to get here, I didn't realize my arms were exposed.

Kyell has been my best friend since we moved to Seattle. I was five when my stepdad, Mick, moved us to this gloomy, godforsaken place. And I mean it. I don't think God, if he does exist, resides here at all. It rains almost every day and when we do get sunlight, it is only a few hours a day. Besides the occasional sun rays, it's pretty much cloudy and gray this time of the year. Under these circumstances, someone who suffers from a lack of melanocytes, walks around looking like a Glo Worm—minus the batteries. Mick used to call me that—Glo Worm—when I was younger. I googled it the other day and was very offended, to say the least.

You would think my skin pigment would be a little darker than it is. Someone once asked if I was an albino because of my light hair color and pale skin tone to match.

Yet again, I had to google the word. And to this day, I still can't answer that question. Who knows?

It's embarrassing. I am lucky I met Kyell before I became such a waste of space. If I hadn't, my life would be even more pointless.

When he sees me, his eyes dance. Perhaps today will be a little better because he is in it.

"Hey, trouble-maker. Where have you been?"

I shrug. "My poor excuses for parents didn't bother to wake me up."

He rolls his eyes and grabs me by the hand. My heart leaps into my throat.

Kyell started holding my hand on the way to class in ninth grade, and it has kind of become our thing. His friends tease us about it, still, but we just ignore them. The truth is, I think holding his hand for the past few years is what's gotten me into this mess. My life is complete with him, but I don't think he feels the same way.

Our friendship has become like a common cold to me. Just when I think I'm over it, my feelings for him sneaks back up on me and lingers in my chest. Well, in this case, my heart.

"So, when did it become their responsibility to wake you up, Jozi?"

"Well, you would think they would notice I wasn't awake by the time they left. I mean, isn't that what parents do?"

"I guess."

Usually, we argue all the way to third period, but his attention is on someone a little further up the hall. I gently squeeze his hand.

"What's up, Ky?"

As soon as the last syllable leaves my mouth, I notice what—, or should I say, who—, has caught his attention. Shelly Anderson.

Kyell glances down at me. "So, do you think I should ask her out?"

Shelly and I became friends in second grade. I finally introduced her to Ky in middle school, then we all started to hang out together. Unfortunately, Kyell has developed a thing for her.

One night, the three of us went to see one of those scary ghost documentaries. Kyell insisted on walking us both home afterwards, Shelly first. He walked her all the way to her door. They shared a few words, but I couldn't make out what they were saying, no matter my efforts. When he made it back to me, his cheeks were flushed. He didn't say one word to me the entire walk to my house

My friendship with Shelly hasn't been the same since then. Ky wanting to date her wasn't a surprise, but still devastating. Shelly Anderson is, "dope on all angles," according to Kyell's buddy, Chad. I have come to realize that it means she's pretty, smart, funny, *and* popular.

I can't argue with Chad. Shelly is effortlessly pretty. To make matters worse, she knows and isn't afraid to flaunt it. It's nauseating. Her blemish-free tanned skin is always flawless and ready for a *Vogue* cover shoot. I wonder how she manages to look so effortlessly beautiful all the time.

She must have some idea how I feel about Ky, but I've never verbally shared it with her. It wouldn't matter, anyway. She's different now.

Right before we reach Shelly and her squad, Kyell drops my hand, like discarded trash. He runs his fingers through his pillow-tossed dark hair, then licks his lips.

"What's up, Shelly?"

In passing, I wave, and she gives a warm smile to Kyell. She blushes. "Hi, Ky."

Yup. I don't even exist in her world.

Their eyes linger on each other even after we pass, to the point he's walking backwards to keep up with me. He turns back around half way down the hall and we walk in silence all the way to class. He stops just shy of the door and leans against the wall.

Who am I kidding? Could I blame her. Kyell is gorgeous. He's tall and lean with a crew cut that fades into light sideburns. His trademark jet black hair, when moussed, puts him in the light of Henry Golding. His sharp, dark features, strong jaw line and drawing eyes give him this modelesque vibe. Every move or stare is picture perfect. Honestly, they are a perfect match.

He closes his eyes and inhales deeply, then lets it out slowly.

"Did you see how she looked at me, Jo? Like she knows. Do you think she knows?"

"Uh, yeah! It is blatantly obvious."

He lifts his head and looks at me. "Did you tell her?"

"No, I didn't tell her! That's not my business to tell. Maybe it's those googly eyes you make at her whenever she says your name. Or, maybe it's how you couldn't take your eyes off her just a minute ago!"

I roll my eyes in disgust, but he waves me off.

"Whatever. I don't make eyes at her."

"Uh, yes, *you do*. Look, I have to get to class, and so do you. See you at lunch."

I walk into class—stomach in knots. Last night's dinner lurches as I slide into my desk. I'm an utter failure at this friend thing.

Yeah, sometimes friends become more than friends, but this is different somehow. In a way, I think he shares my feelings. He just has to discover them. The problem is, just like the stereotypical story of friends becoming more than just friends, I am afraid. Afraid of what?

What if I'm wrong, and he doesn't share my feelings?

What if he does, and it doesn't work out?

I rarely eat lunch. Most of the time I buy an order of fries—because that is the only decent thing on the menu— and a coke. Today, I don't even do that. There's this deep sinking feeling in the pit of my stomach. The faint taste of bile in the back of my throat makes me lose my appetite. *Something awful is going to happen today. I can feel it.*

I spot Kyell sitting at our table. Thankfully, he is sitting alone. Chad Baker, Zeem Crawford and Fredrick Lopez will be here any minute now. I look around to see if they are goofing around with some girls at another table. I don't see them. Track season just started and with the way they have been acting lately—goofing off in class, throwing late-night parties on the weekends—they are definitely feeling themselves. Most of the time I hang out with them. Shelly used to make an appearance to chat with us, but since this year started, I am left as the lone girl member of the group.

Over the summer she started hanging out with the kids who whisper and laugh behind my back. She's so busy trying to fit in with them, she brushes it off.

Today, I hope they all are caught up with something else, because I must get my feelings for Kyell off my chest. *Today's the day. Today's the day I tell him how I really feel.*

I flop down next to Kyell, who is chowing down on steamy hot fries.

"How can you eat those like that? The grease is still sizzling on them."

"That's the only way I can eat'em." He wiggles his eyebrows at me. "Aren't you getting any?"

"No. I don't have an appetite."

Under the table, I clasp my hands to keep them from shaking.

"Are you still mad at your…" he dusts his hands off on his pants and air quotes, "horrible parents?"

"Shut-up, Ky. They are awful, no matter how great you think they are."

"Your parents are cool. Especially your dad. I want to be just like him when I grow up."

He nudges me with his elbow showing his pearly white teeth. That goofy expression always makes me smile.

Of course, Kyell would think my parents are great. His parents are a little—harsh—to say the least. He was never allowed to have friends over when we were younger. Just last year, when Kyell caught the flu, was the first time I ever stepped foot near his house. I stopped by to drop off his chemistry book. His dad greeted me at the door. I didn't even get an invite to come inside. Weird.

His mom was born in the Philippines. When she married his dad, she completely immersed herself in the American culture. Kyell practically knows nothing about his heritage. He tells me he's never heard her speak anything but English.

Kyell resents his parents because they're so rigid. I don't blame him. He and my dad get along well, though. He gets away with coming over so much because Micks a lawyer and Kyell has made his parents believe Mick is mentoring him.

Although, Kyell wants to focus solely on track to get a track scholarship. He has no desire to become a lawyer.

"Think about it this way," Kyell says in between bites, "You could have a set of parents who hound you about the 91 you made on your Calculus mid-term."

"Well, at least you know they care."

"Jo, it's my junior year, and they already have me applying for colleges."

I hold up my hands in surrender. "Okay—okay. You have me beat?"

In minutes, he has scoffed down the entire basket of fries.

I watch him inhale his lunch, trying to think of a way to express what I feel, but the words aren't coming to me.

Instead I ask, "Do your parents keep things from you?"

"I don't know. Maybe. Why?"

"The twins know more about what goes on in our family than I do. It's like my parents don't trust me or something."

He cuts his eyes over at me, "Could it be that you are so shut off from them that they just don't think you would care?"

"Shut up, Ky."

"Exactly my point. Jo, you can't expect them to make you talk to them. You close yourself off."

I fold my arms and begin looking around the lunch room for the guys.

"Just because Mick isn't your real dad, doesn't mean he loves you any less." He looks down at his now empty lunch tray. "My dad acts like I'm one of his soldiers. I hated when he retired because I knew he would miss that life and try to relive it with me. I am literally a cadet in his army."

My attention is drawn back to him with the sudden change in his tone.

"There's no comparison here, Jo. Your parents get the 'Parents of the Year Award.'"

Zeem, Chad, and Fredrick approach and—I fidget on the bench. *You idiot.* Why didn't I seize the opportunity? Chad and Fredrick take a seat on the other side of the table, but Zeem sits next to me.

Chad teases, "Yo, Zeem, no worries. Girls are digging nerds these days."

Immediately, Kyell tunes in to what they are talking about and cracks up right along with them.

Chad—blonde hair blue eyes—is the funniest person I know. His eruptive sense of humor always lands him in trouble. In-school suspension is pretty much his home away from home.

Fredrick Lopez, the son of real estate tycoon, Ricardo Lopez. He sits back with his chill demeanor, smiling, but not laughing, just taking it all in. He has always been the conscience of the group—so analytical. At least that's why I think he takes a back seat in every conversation—he's too busy analyzing us.

And then there's Zeem. Tall, dark, and handsome. Zeem is brilliant. He has the GPA and early ACT scores to prove it. Although he's smart, he hates to flaunt it. In fifth grade he stopped showing up for honors day. He would always make up some excuse about being sick. Our eighth-grade teacher, Mrs. Newman wasn't aware that he was notorious for being absent on honors day. She chose Zeem to give the opening speech at the ceremony, an honor given to the student with the highest GPA, but Kyell had to take his place.

Today Zeem's wearing glasses, and Chad just can't get over his new accessory.

"Hi, guys!" Shelly flashes a grin and leans on the table.

I jump at her high-pitched voice. Where did she come from?

"Oh, sorry I startled you, Jozi."

Chad and Kyell are laughing loudly at Zeem. Apparently, for the past two weeks they have been trying to get him to ask Rowan Backskill to prom. But, he doesn't seem interested.

"Are you afraid she's going to squish you, Zeem," Chad teases.

Zeem ignores him and moves a little closer to me.

"Save me please," he mouths. An aroma of fresh linen and citrus fill the space between us. I shoot him a coy smile.

There's no way Zeem, probably the best-looking guy at Clear View—aside from Kyell, will go out with Rowan Backskill. I mean, she's pretty and all—the glowing red locks draped down her back give her a much softer look—, but she's a massive girl. Not in the heavy sense of the word, but in height. She's basically a girl giant.

To make it worse, lately she's quickly gone from someone who was easy to get along with, to a sarcastic hot head.

I block their conversation out because I am too focused on the dialogue happening between Shelly and Kyell.

"So, Ky. What have you been up to," Shelly asks.

Kyell looks over at her and gives her one of his serious smiles. One side of his mouth is curled up, forming a perfect dimple. I adore his infectious smile. Jealousy, burns like ice cold Coco Cola going down.

Shelly stops and tosses her auburn beach waves to one side of her face, winking at me.

"Hey, Jozi, can you give Ky and I a moment. I really have to talk to him about something personal. It really will only take a sec."

Kyell looks over at me and kind of shrugs his shoulders.

Of course. I'm getting dumped for his crush. I roll my eyes.

"Sure. Take your time."

A sly smile forms on her face. "Thanks."

As I walk away, Zeem grabs my wrist.

"Want some company?"

"No. Not really."

I go out into the courtyard area, where the clouds have overtaken the sun. There's a small glimmer of sunlight unwilling to relent.

I find a spot on the stone wall outlining the perimeter of the courtyard. An oak tree provides additional shade to a few students on their cell phones texting each other. I suck my teeth at the millennial stereotype we always seem to prove valid.

Then, just like the hypocrite I am, I check my hoodie pocket for mine, but it's not there. I must have left it at home in the mad rush to school.

Birds chirp in the trees, annoyingly cheerful considering the conversation playing out in my head between Shelly and Kyell.

One thing is for sure, if the conversation does lead to something more between them, I will most definitely lose him. I can't stand hearing him talk about her or even smelling like her.

My throat closes up and I swallow hard. *Think about something else.*

Kyell is right. I do shut my parents out. I have a right to. All they care about are their jobs and those two selfish brats. I shut everyone out except for him. My heart beats for him. He's my safe place.

For all I know, Miss. Seattle is in there asking him out, because that's what girls do these days. Everyone around me walks by, oblivious to how miserable I am feeling. Clueless of what my mind is contemplating—which, for once, makes me feel powerful. They can't imagine how eager I am to put an end to this torment.

I'm just a little too late. Maybe if I weren't such an emotional wreck, I would have told Kyell how I felt sooner. Maybe, then, I could have been the one he's sitting next to right now, showing off one of his beach boys smiles.

Or, maybe if I had shared my feelings with Shelly. Would she have taken them into consideration? A bitter scream rises up from the pit of my stomach—*Why does it matter?* Who am I to deserve *anyone's* attention?

I'm INVISIBLE.

2 | Is It Worth It

Two blocks from my house, it starts to pour. Slowly my hoodie and jeans start to feel like twenty pounds of sand. I am soaked from head to toe when I finally reach the front door. I feel around in my cold, stretched-out pocket, and realize I don't have my house keys. I envision them right where I left them—sitting on the corner of my dresser. *Wow Jozi! How dumb can you be? No wonder no one takes you seriously.* If it was possible to kick myself—I would.

No one's home, but I ring the doorbell out of sheer desperation.

Pity and rage pulse inside me. How could I be so stupid? I ease down on the front step. There's no telling when my parents will get home and the twins won't arrive from school for another hour. The rain begins a steady beat on my head. I can almost imagine my golden strands of hair turning into brunette icicles—slowly plastering themselves to my face.

This day can't get any worse.

An hour passes, and the rain slows to a light shower. The twin's bus pulls up by the curb, and they jog up, holding their book bags over their heads. Hannah reaches me first, peering down at me with a look that says, What did you do now, Stupid? Although, she doesn't say anything.

She never speaks first. She prefers to let Hazel do all the talking.

Hazel walks up and drops hers arms down to her sides. Her almost jet black afro bends at the weight and impact of the droplets of rain.

"Why are you sitting here in the rain?"

"Why do you think I'm sitting out here, *in the rain*?"

"I'm not quite sure, but it's kind of dumb." She rolls her eyes, edging closer to the door to get out of the deluge.

"I don't have my key, Hazel. I left it on the dresser this morning when I was rushing to get to school *on time* because *no one* bothered to wake me!"

Hazel exhales deeply. She purposely wears this demeanor of an adult who just had a long day at work and has to deal with her unruly child.

Hannah finally chimes in, her eyes filling with tears. "Dad had an emergency at work. We all had to leave a little earlier this morning."

"Well, great! Something else no one bothered to tell me!"

Hazel glances over her shoulder. "Do you want to go next door to Mrs. Cravic's until mom gets off? We could call her to let her know we are locked out."

Mrs. Cravic is our nosey neighbor, who I can't stand being around for more than a few minutes. She and mom connected during the move. Mrs. Cravic brought over meals while we unpacked and got settled in.

I secretly love when she invites us over for dinner, but she asks too many questions. She reminds me of my grandmother. The twins adore her—probably because she loves to bake. My mom couldn't bake a cookie if Rachel Ray herself stood over her giving specific instructions.

I sigh and glare at Hazel. "Brilliant idea! How about you call mom on your brand-new cell phone. I left my raggedy old thing on the charger this morning."

Hannah and Hazel are annoying and spoiled brats. When they were born, they would cry into the night. My mom walked around with dark blue crescent moons under her eyes for the first year of their lives. But, it's all her fault—and partly Mick's—because they never put them down. For a while, I thought they took showers holding them.

I wish I were an only child.

Sometimes I'm not sure why my mom decided to be a pediatric nurse when she has such a hard time coping with her own kids.

The twins are so excited they almost run over to Mrs. Cravic's house, splashing water on me in the process. It doesn't make any difference. I'm already soaked. I drag my attitude and distain across the street. I will not let Mrs. Cravic break my silence today.

The door flies open within seconds of the first ring. Whooping and hollering about us being in the rain, Mrs. Cravic shrieks when she lays eyes on me.

"Oh! Oh, my! Jo, please come in and get out of those clothes!"

I hate when she calls me Jo. Only my family and Ky have that liberty.

Rolling my eyes, I do as I am told. The twins stumble off into the living room, while I slosh behind Mrs. Cravic to the bathroom. My shoulders slump in cadence at the sound of my squishing wet shoes against the hard wood floor. *If she wasn't so nosey, maybe I would have come over here sooner.*

When I walk into her plush, peaches and cream, bathroom I am careful not to step on the mats. Maybe I should show her some respect for allowing me to change, but her décor is nauseating.

"I will be right back, Jo!" Mrs. Cravic yells from outside the door. "I'm going to get you some dry clothes."

I pull off my shoes and socks, then the heavy hoodie. The jeans take longer, but I sit down on the tub to pry them off. Putting everything in a pile in the tub, far away from the mats, I sit back down on the edge of the tub and take in my surroundings.

My hands are shaking. I clasp them together, almost not feeling them at all. I turn my palms over. My fingers tips look like pale gray raisins. I touch my face to warm them a little.

Minutes later, my entire body begins to shiver. I wrap my arms around my body and yearn for Mrs. Cravic to knock at the door again. Just when I think I'm about to go into hypothermic shock, someone knocks at the door.

"Jozi, I have some old clothes of Jennifer's. She wouldn't mind if you borrowed them."

I open the door, grateful, yet annoyed to have to wear someone else's clothes. I clench my teeth together and force out the words.

"Okay. Thank you."

"No problem," she whispers back.

I assess the clothes, a pair of hot pink socks, some black linen joggers, and a white t-shirt that says, "Glad to Be Me."

Ironic. I would rather be anyone else in the world but *me,* right now.

Standing in front of the mirror, I towel dry my dripping hair. It is a tangled mess. My mom never knew how to deal with coarse, curly hair, so she didn't. As a black woman, she has always worn her hair straight. "Less time and energy," she preached. She saved time alright.

Mom would send me to school with a messy ponytail and she didn't have any advice to give me on how to manage it. She has always chemically processed her hair to get it straight, but insists I wear my hair natural. I really don't get it. Why make me suffer something you're really not willing to deal with yourself?

Just another one of her methods to make my life miserable.

To save time, I throw my thick pale-yellow coils into a tight bun and keep moving.

At my eighth-grade promotion dance, Mom let me get it flat ironed. I walked in, afraid of what everyone would think, but when Kyell saw me, he said my hair looked like warm churned butter. He meant it as a joke, but the description stuck with me. Every now and again I remind myself of that night, just so I can manage looking at myself in the mirror.

I put the clothes on, feeling a lot warmer, with the exception of my wet underwear. Glancing in the mirror once more, my breath catches. I stare at my reflection. The girl staring back at me is a harsh reality of how unbearable my life is.

I gape at the now—deep purple scars decorating my wrists. Some are fresh, and some are very old.

My parents had never bothered to ask why I began wearing hoodies to school every day and around the house last year. Even most of my shirts are all long sleeved. They never noticed until it was too late. When they finally did, the habit had already set in.

I started piercing my skin with a razor—trying to see just how deep I could go before it became unbearable. To this day, Kyell hasn't noticed—at least, I don't think he knows. I don't think I could stand it if he found out.

When my parents found out—thanks to my grandmother telling on me—all they did was find me a babysitter with a Ph.D.—Dr. Brasser. She is probably as messed up as I am.

If I go out there like this, Mrs. Cravic will definitely notice. What would I tell her? I went rock climbing? Or the cat—which, we don't own—attacked me?

After about fifteen minutes, a knock comes to the door again.

"Jozi, it's Hannah. Are you coming out? Mrs. Cravic's baking cookies!"

"Uh—…in a minute."

I gather my wet clothes in my arms and decide to use them as a temporary covering. I walk out into the hallway slowly. Mrs. Cravic peeks around the corner from the kitchen

"Go into the laundry room and dump your things into the washer. If you are still a little chilly, you can grab the robe hanging on the bedroom door."

I'm saved. "Okay."

"Help yourself." She gives me one of those warm smiles that reminds me of my grandmother.

I hurry to put the robe on and wrap it tightly around me. I'm hidden again. Safe, for now.

***

This past summer the twins and I spent the entire month of June with Grandma Ellis. My mom wanted the twins to get to know her a little better, since we hadn't visited much in the past few years. Grandma Ellis had been my favorite person in the entire world—up to the day she betrayed me.

I had recently started cutting after watching this reality show about a teenage girl who was suicidal. She had already attempted to end her life twice but was unsuccessful. The third time, she was found on her bedroom floor by her six-year-old brother.

When she was revived by the paramedics and forced to face everyday life again, the weight of shame caused her to regret the decisions. She decided to write the production company to share her story—in hopes of saving other teens' lives.

At that point, I wasn't suicidal, but the story was intriguing. I found myself relating to this girl's family and school issues. She talked about how it all started. How she learned about cutting from a close friend. She would hide away after a rough day at school, or after an argument with her mom and pierce just the first layer of skin. She said it would rid her of all frustrations and anger.

"It was soothing," she said. She said it made her feel like she was in control of at least some aspect of her life. "My life was now an invisible entity that only I could rule and navigate."

Cutting gave her a sense of control and power. She felt like it also gave her a way to control her mom. When her mom made her really mad she would cut even deeper. If she messed around and cut too deep, it would only result in her death and her mom would be to blame for it.

She'd thought this would be her ultimate revenge. But after her little brother

found her that night, she said it wasn't worth it.

"Revenge wasn't worth leaving a taunting image for my brother to relive every day of his life."

I probably watched the recording over twenty times that school year. Just before summer I tried it for the first time. I went into Mick's bathroom and took one of his razors. At first, it was scary. I feared getting caught. I feared the pain. I feared dying.

Eventually, the fear wasn't strong enough anymore. My anger seethed like the lava in a sleeping volcano, ready to erupt after years of dormancy. Anger dominated my fear. The anger and frustration I felt began to make me numb to all things physical and emotional. I held on to my anger, like it was a close friend.

After a few months, I no longer cared about getting caught, about the pain, or—dying. Dying would be my great escape from all of it. My great revenge.

One day we all decided to take a swim in the marina behind Grandma Ellis' house. Stupidly, I forgot that I had cut a few weeks prior. My mom had worked overtime, which caused her to miss my last band performance of the year. She hadn't made any of my performances and she promised not to miss this one.

I was so angry with her; I went back on the vow to never cut again. It was an addiction and I lacked the ability to control it.

The night after the performance, my mom and I had the biggest argument we'd had in a while. I told her I was quitting band, I threw my trumpet case across the kitchen floor and I stormed to my room, locking the door behind me. I cut deeper than I had ever cut before.

The wounds were still very fresh once we got to Grandma's house, but I had completely forgot they were there. Hazel, Hannah and I were all heading out the back door when Grandma Ellis nonchalantly pulled me back into the house.

"Go ahead, Hannah and Hazel, we'll be right out."

I frowned at her. "What's up Grandma?"

Gaping down at my forearms and slowing turning them, she looked deep into my eyes.

"What is going on with your arms, Jo?"

Ashamed, I snatched my arms back. "Nothing, Grandma."

I couldn't think of a suitable lie, let alone a lie at all. I had never lied to her. We were so close, then, I had no problem sharing my deepest secrets with her.

But this was one was too shameful.

She pressed and pressed until I gave in and finally told her the truth. She promised not to tell Mick or the twins, but she insisted on telling my mom. I was livid. I knew my mom wouldn't keep it from Mick—not one second would go by without her texting or calling him about it.

I threatened to never speak to her again if she did, but she didn't care. Grandma Ellis told anyway. Of course, my mom felt it important to tell Mick. I don't think they ever told the twins, but they took several embarrassing precautions after finding out.

They attempted to rid the house of every sharp object. Mick bought an electric razor. My mom bought some of those fancy plastic knives and hired Dr. Brasser. They didn't punish me, but having to see Dr. Brasser every other week is punishment enough.

Mrs. Cravic gets under my skin at times because she reminds me so much of Grandma Ellis—maybe it's because I miss her so much. Sitting up late at night sharing my stories with her was always my escape.

Now we don't talk. I don't have anyone, except Kyell. But I can't talk to Kyell about Kyell. Grandma Ellis always let me talk freely about him. I don't know. My life just seems to get more and more messy by the hour.

3 | Everything is Not as It Seems

When mom finally arrives, she actually looks angry—whether because she had to come home earlier than normal or because of something that happened at work, I don't know.

She loves her job and puts in overtime whenever necessary. I mean, hey, why come home on time when your kids are in school for seven hours a day and you have a live-in babysitter?

That's me, by the way.

When I get home from school, my responsibilities are to cook dinner and, make sure the twins get their homework done, get a bath, and are in the bed by 7:30. On top of all of that, I need to make sure I keep my grades up because I am going to med-school—well that's what they decided I am doing.

Well, none of that happened because we were locked out. But if she tries to blame this on me, I'm going to let her have it. We would have never been locked out if someone would have bothered to wake me up this morning.

I really don't get my mom sometimes. She seems to care more about other people's kids than her own. Once she brought home a baby whose drug-addicted mom put her in a dumpster. She volunteered to be the caretaker while Child

Protective Services found the nearest living relative of the child.

It was so stupid of her. She got all attached to the baby, so when they finally found the child's aunt, she cried and ignored us for months.

Mrs. Cravic smiles genuinely, and she and my mom chat it up for a few minutes. Then, awkwardly, they both walk into the kitchen and begin to whisper. I look over at them and notice they are looking over at me.

I feel exposed. A cold chill slithers down my spine. They're talking about *me*. Within seconds, they hug. My mom locks eyes with me. She quickly walks by like I have done something wrong and she's trying to avoid my gaze.

The rain stopped hours a-go, so when we walk out into the humid spring air, the moon has finally taken its rightful place, setting an ominous tone for the night.

"Bye, girls! Goodbye, Nicole," Mrs. Cravic calls out.

I catch up to my mom. "What were you two talking about?"

She hands Hazel the keys. "Run on home and get washed up."

She looks over her shoulder, just as Mrs. Cravic is closing her door. She stops in the middle of the road, watching the twins as they run ahead of us.

Our street is quiet. The glow of the moon reflects off the asphalt, giving it a glossy look. She walks slowly over to the sidewalk. When the twins are in the house, she turns to face me.

I ask again, more forcefully, "What were you two talking about?"

"We were talking about YOU," she almost yells out.

I take a step back. What right does she have to be angry at *me*?

"Why? What were you talking about?"

My mom tends to be calm in most situations, so her attitude and demeanor are a little alarming to me. Her face is contorted, and she seems angry. *At me*! Now, I find myself getting even more heated because I have no idea what I have done, and I am the one who should be angry right now.

"Look, Jo, I have had a rough day and I don't need this right now." She points a demanding finger at the house. "So, straighten up your attitude, get in there, change out of Jennifer's clothes, and get ready for dinner."

My heart beats faster. I can hear it pulsing in my ears. and I bite my bottom lip to keep from exploding. How could her day of changing diapers and bathing babies be compared to mine. How could she speak to me this way after the day I've had?

"I know you told her my secret—and if you have, mom, I will never forgive you. I will find out if she knows, and if she does know, I won't be able to bear the sight of you."

I walk into the house and shut the door behind me.

What could she possibly be so upset about?

That look in my mom's eyes was something I have never seen.

✳❧❀❧✳

As much as I hate our family dinners, I go down to join them after I have changed into my own clothes. I am starving after skipping breakfast and lunch today, so I might as well tolerate them all for a little while longer.

Mick is sitting at the table reading from a manila folder with laser focus, while the twins are playing rock-paper-scissors over who will get to choose the show they watch after dinner. My mom is prepping a salad at the sink when I take my seat.

Mick looks up. "How was your day, Light Bright?" He gives me a small smile.

Usually, when he asks, "How was your day," it doesn't mean he really wants to know. If I really begin to tell him, he looks at me like he's listening, then, hHHhHis eyes glass over, his mind's edsexsomewhere else. After my freshman year of high school, I gave up trying to answer that question. Now, I just say, "It was okay."

"I heard you were locked out for over an hour after school."

I slump into my chair. "Please, don't get me started, Dad."

Mom walks over and places the salad bowl on the table, "Yeah, please, don't get her started."

My mom and got Mick married when I was only four. He adopted me shortly afterwards and I have willingly called him dad ever since. He knows trouble when he sees it.

His eyes grow big. "O—kay." He turns his attention to the twins. "How was your day, girls?"

Hazel is mouthing VICTORY when I look over in their direction. As usual, Hazel answers.

"Great!"

"How was your day, Hannah?"

Hannah looks down at the plate mom just sat in front of her, as if searching for answers.

"What's the matter, honey?" Mick raises his eyebrows, "You can watch your show after Hazel watches hers."

"No, it's not that."

Mom stops dead in her tracks. "Then, what is it, honey?"

She sounds so concerned and motherly. It's nauseating. Maybe I'm not hungry for dinner after all.

Hannah's eyes well up with tears.

"Can I be excused?"

"Sure, honey." Mick frowns after her as Hannah flees the kitchen.

Mom follows right behind her. Sobs escape Hannah's mouth as she climbs the stairs. The three of us pray and begin eating, in silence. Just the way I like it.

Hannah is such a cry-baby.

After dinner, I help Hazel clean up and put the food away. And, just like the little responsible brat she is, Hazel fixes a plate for Hannah and takes it up to her room when we finish.

Mom and Hannah never come back down. I sit with Hazel for just a few minutes—because I am required to—and then head up to my room. What could be so horrible that when asked about school today, Hannah begins to cry? I brush the thought away and flop down on my bed. I stare up at my dull pink ceiling.

When I was in fourth grade, I begged my mom to let me change the color of my walls to pink. The twins hadn't come, yet, and I was still into pastels and all things princess. The white castle decals and pink glittery tiaras have come down, but the stale pink color of my walls remain. Repainting my room is way overdue.

My phone buzzes. I look to my right and there it is—still on my night stand connected to the charger. Just where I left it.

I pull the charging cord out, only to find I have seven text messages. Three are from my mom. She was checking in on me before she found out I was at Mrs. Cravic's. Since I am on suicide watch she checks in three times a day—like clockwork. But I know it's because she was told to do it.

The other four texts are from Kyell.

Where are you?

Are you home yet?

Are you okay?

Please call me as soon as you get home.

I text him as soon as I finish reading them.

Jo: *Hey, Ky. I am fine. I left my phone at home today.*

...

Ky: *Ugh, thank God you are okay! You had me worried sick, Girl!*

Jo: *Whatever, you don't care.*

Ky: *If I didn't, I wouldn't even bother.*

My heart beats a little faster and all I can see are his soft brown eyes staring down at me. I smile for the second time all day, fully aware that he is the reason for both.

Ky: *Are you there?*

Jo: *Yeah, I'm here.*

Ky: *So, Shelly didn't come to talk about what I thought*

Jo: *What did she want*

Ky: *She wanted me to be her partner on our chemistry project! Can you believe that?*

Yeah, I actually can. Everybody knows Ky is super smart when it comes to science or math. Zeem is better, but he's not in our chemistry class.

I can also believe that she wanted to beat me to the punch. But I don't care. School is the last thing I want to think about right now.

Jo: Well, whoopee!

Sarcasm overload.

Ky: Save your sarcasm, Jo.

Ky: Are you mad? I know we talked about being partners, but this could be my chance, Jo.

Jo: No. We have been partners before. I can find another science nerd to dump all the work on.

Ky: Cool! You are stellar!

Jo: I know.

Ky: See you tomorrow.

Jo: See you tomorrow.

Ky: By the way, tell your dad I want to come by tomorrow night.

Jo: For what?

Ky: Just tell him. He will be fine with it.

Surprisingly, I am not mad that Shelly asked Kyell to be her partner for the project. I am relieved. Relieved that I was wrong, and their conversation wasn't about what I thought it was about.

A light knock rattles my door and it creaks a little when my mom peeks her head in—without permission, of course.

"Hey, Jo. Can I come in?"

I turn on my side to gaze at my lovely pale, pink wall. "Sure. It's your house."

She sits down next to me.

"Jo, I'm sorry for being so—so blunt with you today. Today was rough for all of us. I won't go in-to detail, but just know, your dad may be in need of a few more hugs than usual. Well, considering that you don't give out many these days, just try to be kind."

She rubs my arm. "I snapped because I didn't want you bringing that attitude into the house when so much is going on already."

Mick is a lawyer. One of the best in the state. He's never lost a case. One day, last week, he came home with a bottle of sparkling cider and gifts for all of us. He had just won the "biggest case of his life,"—his words. Maybe he's reached the glass ceiling and hasn't realized it yet, I'm not sure, but he still works just as hard as any rookie.

I don't say a word, but she continues, "Then, Hannah. My poor little girl." She sighs.

What about me? That's what I want to say, but I don't. I try to hold my silence to make sure this whole sob story ends sooner.

"Honey, I love you so much. I don't like you being so distant. Please, say something. I know things aren't easy for you, but if you don't talk about your problems, there's nothing I can do."

I am emotionless. She doesn't really care. If she did she would be home a lot more. Nothings changed since they discovered that I'm a cutter. I mean yes, they have gotten rid of the sharp objects, but other than that, I am still invisible.

She tugs on my shoulder.

"Talk to me, honey."

"Mom, I have nothing to say."

She sighs. "Just know, whenever you are ready, I am here for you."

I roll my eyes. *Yeah, right.*

Finally, she stands up and bends down to kiss me on my cheek. I hear her footsteps leave my room then the door shuts.

4 | A World on Fire

No one will ever convince me that what I learn in chemistry class will help me in the real world. Not that learning chemistry is useless, but it's pointless to me. The only reason I enjoy coming to this agonizing class is because it's the only class I share with Ky. Unfortunately, Shelly and some of her gang are in this period, too.

What makes a class "stellar"—according to Kyell—is the teacher. I have had many lousy teachers in my day, but Ms. Shultz, is the winner of the "Worst Teacher of All Time" award—hands down. She's short and stout, just like a little tea pot, but more like one of those hand-me-down kettles from the first group of settlers. Her hair isn't really hers— well, I guess it is because she bought it, but she wears this awful bob. It's always crooked. To top it all off, she speaks as if she is from an old Mr. Bean episode. And, when she yells at us her neck jiggles like a roster getting ready to crow. This makes for an remarkably interesting start of my day.

On one of her good days she shared with us that she grew up in Chicago and went to an inner-city school. I guess she was trying to relate to the darker skinned population in the classroom, but we weren't buying it, just like we didn't buy the fake British accent she uses off and on to sound sophisticated. Most days, she is ten minutes late to class. No one reports it because hey, who cares. She always seems to have too much going on.

Today, Ms. Shultz stumbles into class, late as usual, carrying a large satchel in one hand and a stack of papers in another. Out of breath, she slings the mess onto her desk and begins to diligently unpack her satchel. As she is notorious for, she unpacks and organizes, for what seems like forever, never acknowledging us until she has finished with what *she* is doing. Meanwhile, students are laughing at her, whispering to each other, texting on the phones, or trying to get their homework done.

Usually, I sit right behind Ky. Today, since he and Shelly have become partners on the project Ms. Shultz assigned, I sit as far away from them as I can. This way I can't see or hear anything about this budding romance.

When Ky finally arrives, I lock eyes with him just as Rowan Backskill slams her books down on my desk.

"Why are you in my seat, Skies?"

Ms. Shultz doesn't seem to notice the commotion. She never does when there's someone making it difficult for me.

"Can you sit over there?" I point to an empty seat right next to me, "I don't think we have assigned seating in this class."

Rowan, doesn't falter.

"Skies, if you don't get out of my seat, I am going to make you wish you didn't wake up this morning.

Too late.

I don't move, nor do I make eye contact. Students are noticing. The whispers seem to die down as Kyell walks over to us.

"Okay." Rowan's eyes flash a glint of satisfaction. "Since you won't move, I'm going to tell everyone your pitiful little secret."

Rowan has never been someone that I liked, but she has recently become a "mean girl." It seems that with each passing day, she becomes more bitter. I am not sure why she walks around with a such a huge chip on her shoulder, lately. And, even more odd, she and Shelly have become close friends.

I try peering past her to see if Ms. Shultz is finished yet.

Rowan's tall with a physique like that of a pro wrestler—but girly at the same time. She's beautiful in her own way, smart, and lately angry. Really angry. Why does she insist on sitting here, in this specific seat today? It beats me, but I am not in the mood to be bullied. Not today—not now—or ever again.

Rowan scowls at me once more. "Get up!"

What could she possibly know about me? I never talk to her—I never talk to anyone at Clear View. But, the thought of her knowing my secret does kind of scare me. I am still unmovable.

"What secret?" I let a triumphant smirk cross my face.

She grins back at me, turning around to see if she has an audience.

"Rowan, get a life."

I peek around Rowan's tall frame again. Hoping Ms. Shultz is finished organizing. She isn't.

Ky questions, "What's up, Rowan?"

Ky always shows up when I have gotten myself into something thick and muddy. He's always been my defender. I am pretty good at handling myself, yet I find comfort in the thought he cares enough to join me in my mess.

"Helmer, tell your charity case to get up—NOW—before I set her whole world on fire."

It's funny she says that because it's all I can see right now. Flames blazing up from my chest. I squint my eyes at the heat.

"Look, Rowan, there's a seat right over there." Kyell shrugs. "Why can't you just go over and sit there?" Across the room, I glimpse Shelly's smug face. She has done a 180 to see the action. The entire class is quiet now. My instincts are telling me to just jump up and punch Rowan's face in, but I don't. Instead, I smile. I give her the biggest smile I can possibly manage and lean back in my seat.

"This is not your seat." I speak through my teeth, rage pulsing through me. I'm tired of being ignored and pushed around.

Rowan smiles right back at me and looks around at our audience.

"That's okay, Skies, I don't want to push you over the edge. You are a delicate case. Why don't you tell everyone why you are always wearing that smelly hoodie even when it's hot outside—during gym class—when the AC is out? It must smell like a corpse underneath that thing."

She pinches her nose in time to get a gasp out of the crowd. I ball my hands into fists. Ready to give her what she is begging me for.

"Go ahead," her eyes glint with victory, "tell them how you have cut up your arms. Show them those slabs of meat. You are a joke, Skies! Your only friend in the world only hangs out with you because he feels sorry for you."

Rowan points at Kyell. "He thinks you will shatter at any moment, so he only wastes his time with you because he doesn't want to be the reason you finally decide to end your pitiful little life."

My eyes lock on Ky. His face is emotionless. I can't tell if he agrees or if he is just as hurt as I am. I can see in his eyes that he knew. He knew about the cutting. My entire body is a-blaze.

I fly out of the seat. Everything turns into a red blur.

I can't see. I can only feel. I feel my fists pounding into Rowan.

I hear voices chanting—FIGHT—FIGHT!

Then, I black out.

5 | Revenge

When I break through the surface of the blackness, I am in Principal Donovan's office. I quickly look around. I don't see him, but my mom is sitting right next to me, rambling on about how much trouble I'm in.

I can't make myself look at her. The blaze still burns in my chest and sitting next to her is only stoking the fire. She is the only one, other than Grandma Ellis and Mick, who knew my secret.

I jump to my feet. "Did you tell anyone else!"

She pulls at my arm, but I snatch it away.

"Jo, please have a seat. You are already in enough trouble. Mr. Donovan should be coming back any minute now."

My breathing picks up. I look down at my shaking hands. They're covered in blood.

"Oh, my God! Mom, what did I do?"

"You broke her nose, that's what you did. Now we just have to pray Mr. Donovan doesn't expel you. I can't imagine you being homeschooled without supervision during the day."

Normally, hearing her say something so selfish would upset me. The fact my hands are covered in someone else's blood, and all she can think about is how this will inconvenience her life. Typical.

My head starts to spin. I slowly sit down and try to remember all that happened, but I can't. It's a blur. I lost control completely. My heart feels like someone or something has gripped it. My breathing catches.

"Is she okay?" I ask.

Before she can answer, Mr. Donovan walks in and takes a seat behind his desk. He exhales deeply and stares up at the ceiling for several minutes. He finally looks at my mom with soft eyes and begins speaking directly to her.

"Mrs. Skies, because of the seriousness of this situation, I am going to have to take action. Jozi will not be held completely accountable for what took place today, but she will have to deal with the consequences for her actions."

My mom leans forward in her chair. "What do you mean by she won't be held 'completely accountable?'"

Mr. Donovan looks over at me, regret in his eyes, "Well, Ms. Shultz was in the classroom the entire time this incident was taking place." He looks back over at my mom, "Several students can attest to this. Knowing Jozi is one of our students who is at risk—" I shift in my seat, "—she should have been more attentive."

"I see." My mom looks at me in shock, then back at Mr. Donovan.

She reaches over for my hand, and I push it away.

Mr. Donovan frowns at me. "There are some consequences Jozi, even though you were extremely provoked."

My mom looks over at me. I can tell she's crying, because her voice cracks when she replies.

"We understand."

I don't care. She hasn't been through what I have been through today. And if it were up to her, she would still be at work—with her other family, as she calls them.

Mr. Donovan leans on his desk. "I am going to suspend you for five days, Jozi. I am sorry for what happened today, but no matter the circumstance, physical violence should never be your first choice."

Rolling my eyes. "Are we done?"

"No." He turns his attention to my mom. "Jozi must have a signed release form from Dr. Brasser before she can return."

"Yes." My mom nods, "I will make sure she is seen."

He looks back at me, "Now, we are done."

⚜

On the way home, I play every scenario of how my secret got out, over—and over—again. There's no figuring it out and asking my mom will only send me into another fit of rage. I just want to lose it, but I try to hold it together, at least until we get home—and I'm alone.

It feels like my body is caving into itself. The cold grasping arms of darkness are begging to close me in, but I keep them at bay. With clenching teeth, I lean my head on the window.

My mom is rambling on about how kind Mr. Donovan was to only suspend me for five days. She asks questions about Ms. Shultz, but I drown her out.

Five days? I wish he would have expelled me. I can't go back there. I won't go back there. Why can't this all just be a bad dream. It sucks this is my reality on a regular basis. Never a sliver of light. Nothing but dark, gray days.

By now the entire school knows!

I replay Rowan's words in my head until I have them memorized. I catch a replay of Ky's eyes and they cut right into my soul. My heart quakes in my chest and my entire body is shaking. I can't go back there. I will never be able to face any of them again.

When we pull into the driveway, my mom presses the lock button before I can get out.

"What are you doing, Mom?" I throw my head back in frustration. "Please. I can't do this right now."

"No," she says calmly, "Not until you speak to me."

"I have nothing to say to you, Mom."

"Well, I have something to say to *you*." She examines her hands. She does that when she's upset. "Jozi, I have no idea how that young lady knew all of those things about you. I promise I don't. I would never do anything to hurt you. All I have ever wanted was to keep you safe. Everything I keep from you is for your safety. I don't want you to have one extra thing on your plate."

"I don't get it, but whatever," I snap.

"Sweetheart, there are somethings you don't know because it's best to keep it that way."

"You know what, Mom. I am sick and tired of you and dad keeping things from me. It's like you think I am a fragile little egg that's going to crack at the slightest touch. You tell the twins more than you tell me and I am sick of it!"

I make a quick advance at the unlock button and I am out of the car before she can lock it again.

I stay in my room for the remainder of the day. She never goes back to work so that she can keep an I on me. A warm sense of gratification fills me at the thought of her being somewhere she doesn't want to be. Home.

When she knocks at my door around six to see if I want dinner, I tell her, "I would rather starve."

Around 6:30 my phone buzzes. It's Ky.

Ky: Hey, Jo. How R U?

I don't respond.

Ky: I heard you were suspended and not expelled. Turns out Donovan does have a heart.

Ky: Don't' worry about anything. I will get all the work you will miss and bring it to you tomorrow.

Ky: Come on, Jo. Answer me...

Ky: I guess I'm not coming over tonight to talk LAW with your dad. See you tomorrow?

An hour or so later the questions I have for him begin to haunt me.

Jo: Did you know this entire time?

A few minutes pass before he answers.

Ky: Yes.

Jo: How?

Ky: Your dad told me. Please don't tell him I told you. He loves you so much. He wanted me to keep an eye on you...

Jo: So how did Rowan find out? Did you tell her?

Ky: No.

Ky: But, I did tell Shelly. Only because she noticed some changes in you, too. She was worried.

Jo: Wow...

I throw my phone against the wall. It doesn't shatter but the screen cracks, and the sound gives me a small dose of gratification. Night comes and I fill my pillow with shouts of rage. Tears fall until there's nothing left. I drift off to sleep, contemplating revenge.

They all deserve what's coming to them—my mom, Kyell, Shelly, Rowan, and Mick. Especially Mick.

6 | Biological Father

You would think my real dad would have tried to find me by now—but—he hasn't. You would think I would be satisfied with the dad I have—but—I'm not. The feeling of not being wanted finds a way to haunt you.

It finds a way to make you feel like you aren't good enough—like you aren't valued, so you work to try and fill the void with other things.

For me, Mick filled the void for a while. But who am I kidding? He's not my biological father. He's just a man who pays the bills and is too busy to *see* me.

My mom never even told me his name, my biological father, I mean. Sometimes, when I am asleep, I see him—in my dreams. While still unconscious, I rub my eyes ferociously to clear my blurry vision. My eyes are like an out of focus camera. I adjust. I blink, but nothing.

His face is locked away in my memories. Somewhere out there, I hope he remembers *my* face.

7 | Making a Run for It

The next morning, my mom retrieves the little metal key above my door post and unlocks my door. Before I was put on suicide watch those little metal keys where put up somewhere. Now, they are everywhere around the house. I don't bother trying to hide them anymore, nor do I try throwing them away, because they just keep reappearing.

When she comes in, I am already awake, sitting up against my headboard.

"Oh, you're awake. I thought you would still be asleep, since you don't have school and all."

I don't say anything. I keep my eyes focused on the small cork board right above my desk. In the center is a picture of Kyell and me. I had been staring at it for hours before she walked in.

"Well, since you seemed to be dressed and ready for the day, I am escorting you over to Mrs. Cravics'. She will be keeping you company during your suspension. Tomorrow, you have an appointment with Dr. Brasser."

On the inside, I just want to break down and cry some more, but I hold it together. My anger won't allow me to break down in front of her. Plus, if I broke down, she probably wouldn't leave. I need her to leave. Whether I go to Mrs. Cravics' house or not, I'm going through with my plan.

Scooting to the edge of the bed, I slip my feet into my shoes.

"Oh, by the way, Mr. Donovan called yesterday, shortly after we got home. He had to increase your suspension days to 10 instead of five days. Rowan's parents made a big fuss once they found out you only got five days. I told him that it was understandable." She walks over to me.

"Do you understand?"

I break the silence, and cock my head to one side, "You know what, Mom? I really don't care."

She stares down at me. "You know what, I wish you did. I think if you did care, all of this wouldn't be happening."

"Oh, yeah, because everything's always my fault. You have no idea what I'm going through."

"Because you won't tell me!"

I look at her, she looks at me.

"I'm sorry, Jo, it's just…" she shakes head. "I'll be waiting for you downstairs, Jozi. We have fifteen-minutes before we have to leave."

I wonder what she was about to say, but I don't ask. She walks out the door and I close it behind her. Walking over to my desk, I decide to write some of my thoughts down. Slowly, I pull out the parchment Mick bought me this past Christmas. This was the one gift that made this Christmas better than the ones in the past. I loved it because I thought maybe they did pay attention to me. Writing has always been my escape. I hate clacking away on a computer, but it's something about letting the ink flow onto a crisp piece of parchment. Writing it all down frees me in a way.

Now, they will hold the stain of my shame. I put pen to paper and I let my emotions bleed on to the creamy surface.

Mrs. Cravic busies herself making breakfast, while I silently take a seat in the living room, my escape plan playing out in my head. As I decide on how I'm going to make a run for it, my eyes widened at the realization of Mrs. Cravic's mammoth wall to wall, floor-to-ceiling bookcase.

I marvel at the fixture and without realizing, I'm moving directly towards it. I run my fingers over the spines, just mesmerized at how beautiful and big this room has become.

"Some of those books are decades and decades old, you know. Some of them were passed down to me from great aunts, great uncles…" Mrs. Cravic wipes her hands on a towel tucked into her powder blue apron.

"You can borrow one at any time. Hey, borrow more than one. I have read them all!" She laughs.

I walk back over to the couch. "No thank you. I have my own books."

"Okay. Suit yourself. Just let me know if you change your mind and decide to stop being so stubborn."

I blink at her blunt remark. "Huh?"

She walks over to the recliner and exhales as she sits down.

"Yeah, I said it. You are stubborn. Why don't you try using that strong will of yours to get what you want?"

"You have no idea what I want."

"Well, you are mad with your mom and dad because they work more than they are at home."

I shift my weight in the couch to face the window. Just like I said. Nosey.

"You despise the twins because they get all the attention when your parents *are* at home. You are upset with your grandmother because she cares enough about you to share you issues with your mom."

I glare at her. I knew it. She has known all this time. What liars they all are.

"You hate your biological father because he hasn't tried to reach out to you. And you loath Kyell because you don't have the guts to tell him how you really feel about him."

Raw anger runs rapid through my body.

"You feel alone, like no one sees you. So, you're angry, but being angry isn't going to fix any of your problems. Be angry is only going to hold you in a prison that no one but yourself has the key to."

Standing to my feet, I blurt out, "Would you just be quiet! You know all of this about me because you're just a nosey old lady!"

She folds her arms across her chest. "Call me what you want, but I care about you. I care about your entire family. "

"Well, I don't care about you—or, any of them!"

She sits forward in her chair and repeats the same ridiculous statement she said earlier. "Try using that will of yours to get what you want."

Still standing, I flinch at her closeness.

"Tell your mom and dad how you feel. They work so hard because they only want to give you girls all the things they never had. And spend some time with the twins. Get to know them. Stop focusing so much on yourself.

I try to interrupt. "I do not…"

"Talk to your mom about your feelings about your biological father. Dig a little. Maybe then you will have some closure."

"What do you know about…" At this point I just want to smack her. I walk over to the window, turning my back to her, but she continues.

"And either tell Kyell how you feel or move on. You have your entire life ahead of you, he's not the only boy on the block."

"You don't know anything about me! And everything isn't as easy as you make it seem."

I clinch my teeth. "Just because you ignore the fact that your husband is never home doesn't mean everyone can go around ignoring things in their lives! So, shut up and stay out of my business!"

I storm off to Jennifer's old room before she can respond. I lock the door behind me, hoping she doesn't try to make entry. On the dresser, an old stereo catches my attention. I press the on-button and gush with a strand of happiness because a little green light flashes. An old Backstreet Boys song is playing.

A knock comes to the door.

"Jo, I'm sorry. I was only trying to help. Please come out and have breakfast. Your mom said you really need to eat."

I turn the volume up and blast the music as loud as it can go. Checking to see if my cell phone and the knife I stole from Mrs. Cravic's kitchen are still in my pocket, I escape from the bedroom window and make a run for it.

8 | Adar'el

When I arrive at school, the campus seems empty. Classes have already started for the day, and there's not a single student in sight. I head to the back of the building to make entry where I know no one will see me. I hop the gate and swiftly walk into the double doors leading to the gym.

Today, I am thankful for Coach Pierce's laziness. He didn't lock the back door of the gym. In the distance the sports health class is running laps. Coach Pierce stands with his back toward me, so I stealthily enter the gym, being careful not to let the door slam shut.

I walk right through the empty gym and take the stairs to the second floor where most of the junior classes are held. I've decided on doing it in the girl's bathroom. It's the place where they write all of the new rumors. On the back of any stall during the week, you could find the juiciest rumors written in black sharpie. Over the weekend, if there are any new writings, the janitors usually paint over them. But this doesn't stop the transcribers from doing what they do best. I'm eager to see if there's anything up about me.

I go into the last stall and lock the door. Surprisingly, there's nothing about me. Then again, they may have spewed their venom in another stall.

It will be a while before my chemistry class starts, so I settle in. I choose to act right before class ends. This way Shelly and her crowd will find me. They always stop by the bathroom to check their hair and make-up after class.

Crouched on the toilet, I begin to feel light-headed as I stare at the dull gray cinder blocks. My blood is pumping so rapidly through my veins I can't catch my breath. I lean my head against the stall and try to calm myself. Even counting down from twenty isn't working.

What I have to do is obvious to me. There's no turning back now. I broke someone's nose. Everyone knows my secret. I was humiliated—in front of Kyell. He pities me. No one wants to have anything to do with me, not even my family. My real father doesn't even care that I exist. There's no way I can stand living this life or another minute in this reality. Once this is done, I won't have to deal with any of this anymore. A dark, uninterrupted sleep is all I long for.

An hour passes. I have gotten probably one hundred phone calls and texts from I don't know who. I don't bother to check because I don't care. They'll get the letter, and everything will become clearer. They will all regret what they have done to me.

The late bell rings which means Chemistry class has just started. I step down out of my crouched position and pull the knife from my hoodie pocket. The adrenaline pulsing through me causes my hand to shake. I fumble around in my hoodie, again, for the pain killers I snuck out of mom's bathroom medicine cabinet. I pop an entire handful into my mouth and step out of the stall to get some water. After several swallows, I finally get them all down, almost choking on the intense taste of the powder left over on my tongue.

Contemplating the pain, I am about to inflict on myself, I hope they dissolve quickly.

Water runs down the side of my mouth, and I wipe it away nicking myself with the knife. I lean forward to look in the mirror and find a small hairline cut right above my lip. *Wow, you can't even do this right.*

After a few minutes, I start to feel like my stomach is turning in on itself. I heave over the sink, gasping for breath. Nothing comes out.

It's either now or a life time of this horror film, Jo. Hiking my sleeves up, I press the knife over my left wrist first. I stare down at it, taking in one more breath.

A bright light casts over my eyes from the reflection of the knife, blinding me. I am accosted with glimpses of faces. Faces of people that ignore me or ostracize me every chance they get. I am locked in time for a moment, then in a flash, they all are gone.

My breath picks up and my hands begin to shake even faster. My heart is beating so fast it almost feels like it has missed some beats. I begin regretting taking the pills. Should I back out, I ponder. A sharp cutting pain shoots through my stomach. Dropping the knife, I heave over the sink again and vomit its contents.

After three violent heaves, I'm finished, out of breath and dizzy. I stand up straight to give some relief to my back, but everything begins to spin. My throat burns from the bile and the pills I took. I fall down to the floor, trying to regain my balance. Right beside me is the knife. Gathering the courage once again, I pick it up and angle the knife right over my left wrist. *If I do it fast, it will be over quickly.*

As I press the blade down into my flesh, once again, a light is cast from the knife, but this time it is even brighter.

Stunned, I drop the knife, but it doesn't matter—the light doesn't let up. It fills the entire bathroom. I feel as though I have stepped into one of those buildings that help ships to find their way. I throw my hand up, blinded once again. After several minutes. The light lifts and from one of the stalls, I hear a subtle sound.

Slow and steady. It almost sounds like a ball hitting a surface. No one has come in—I don't think. Unless... I blacked out from the pills and didn't realize it.

I stand to my feet. Steading myself, I walk slowly to the stalls.

"Is anyone there?" I call out.

Maybe I'm just hallucinating. No one has walked into this bathroom for the hour I've been in here. The pills and my anxiety might be getting the best of me.

The sound is getting louder. I tip toe closer to the stall, hoping that whoever it is will just come out.

"Hello?"

The door swings open and the sound stops. Heavy footsteps echo out of the stall and then—they stop. Sweat beads begin to run down my forehead. I swallow hard. No one walks out, but I can sense someone is there.

"Hello! Who's there?"

Uh, hey, there! Don't be alarmed. I was just stopping in to get some things done before this weekend.

Shaken, and frankly a little frustrated, I call out, "Who's there?"

One second. The toilet flushes. *My name is Adar. Adar'el actually.*

The voice is abstruse, with a wasp of tenderness to it. Slowly, this person steps one foot outside the stall and then the next. Carefully walking towards me, the stranger holds up both hands in front of him. He's a broad-chested man, wearing a v-neck t-shirt and blue jeans that are torn at the knees. In one hand, he's holding a small blue ball. The source of the noise I was hearing. What a weirdo. In the girl's restroom, bouncing a ball. Go figure. The craziness of it all makes me even more freaked out.

Don't be alarmed. I'm not going to hurt you, he says.

He is staring at me. I trace his eyes to the object I'm holding. *The knife!* I quickly look back up at him—thankful he thinks I have the knife to defend myself. He doesn't look like a student here and he's definitely too young to be a janitor—at least, I think.

"Who are you? I have never seen you around here before."

His eyes are serene as he moves slowly towards me, hands still held out, pacifying.

I told you, I'm Adar'el, but you can call me Adar.

"Well, what are you doing in here? This is a girl's bathroom," I protest. And stop moving towards me, or I will scream!"

My voice feels and sounds so small coming out. He doesn't react to my request or answer my question, instead he continues to close in on me. He is a pretty tall guy and his face is—pleasant, but everything in me screams for me to turn around and run.

I don't. As he moves closer and closer, my body tenses up. I can't move. I try to will myself to move, but my feet are like sandbags.

All I can focus on is his eyes. They are like the tide of the Atlantic Ocean—blues and greens of rushing, rolling waves with a hint of tiny embers of light sprinkled throughout.

Easy now, he says, then gently removes the knife from my hand.

"I—I…"

I can't think of a response. I don't want him to find out what I was about to do. The shame of it begins to dig into my chest. He walks over to the door, where a huge trash can has practically just appeared out of thin air. He throws the knife into it and walks back toward me.

"Are—are you a janitor or something?"

I guess you can call me that. There's a myriad of terms for someone who cleans. If you're asking if I clean things up, then, yes.

He straightens his shoulders just a bit, and holds his chin high, making him seem two feet taller.

I also like to think of myself as a defender. Or, a protector.

He lets the last word out rather slowly, letting it drift into the air like a hang glider.

"O—kay."

He smiles which makes him appear a lot less intimidating.

Finally, my legs and feet are working again, but just a little shaky. I take a few steps back, trying to take everything in. Who is this guy?

He begins to bounce that small blue ball again, but this time up into the ceiling. He throws it up swiftly and then catches it with quick precision. It's as if he is waiting for my next question, so I don't keep him waiting.

"What do you mean by protector? Shouldn't you be somewhere cleaning something?"

He stands maybe seven feet tall, his auburn hair almost brushing the ceiling. He doesn't look down at me, his eyes are fixed on the ball. The sound of it bouncing is almost therapeutic.

Then my eyes are drawn to his massive feet. Yes, his feet, which are almost completely bare. He is wearing the most comfortable looking sandals I have ever seen. I laugh at the awkwardness of what he is wearing. I've never seen a man so big dressed like a teenager.

I just did.

"Did what?"

Cleaned something. That's why I'm in here. Something needed to be cleaned and someone needed protection.

Then, like he just got word to move on to the next order of business, he stops bouncing the ball and walks over to the trash can.

Jozi, no more playing with shiny sharp objects, okay? And you better get out of here, the bell is going to ring in seven minutes.

"Wait—what?"

Before I can finish my sentence, he pushes the trashcan out of the door and leaves. I'm dumbfounded for a few seconds, then I am jolted into action.

9 | Where Do We Go from Here?

There have been many situations in my short life where I felt like I was trapped in a dream I couldn't seem to wake up from. Once Grandma Ellis caught Emmerson Sanders and me smooching behind the cherry blossom tree in her backyard. I was only ten and knew I wouldn't see him again after the summer. He wasn't a boy I liked by any means, but I wanted to kiss a boy for the first time, and I was comfortable trying this with him, so I did.

When Grandma came creeping around that tree and my lips were still pressed to Emmerson's chubby, round face, I almost went into cardiac arrest. I hoped with everything it was just a bad dream—but—it wasn't.

Just as I hopped the fence in the back of the school, the bell rang. I guess, *Adare* or whatever his name was, was right.

I got out of the school without being caught, but I worried about the uproar I may have caused at home. It probably took Mrs. Cravic all of five minutes to realize I was no longer there. She called my mom, who probably left work with great hesitation, calling Mick in the process. Knowing Mick, he called the police right after hanging up with mom. My street is probably a three-ring circus right now. How am I going to hide from this?

When I reach Vineyard Way, it is surprisingly empty. I was expecting at least two or three police cars at my house. I contemplate if I should head back over to Mrs. Cravic, but I decide against it and just have a seat on my front porch to process what just happened.

I turn my cell phone back on and it begins to buzz non-stop in my hoodie pocket. I pull it out to see there are over seventy texts in my inbox and still coming in. I scan through them all.

My mom, Mick and Mrs. Cravic have called several times and left messages. The texts are mostly from Kyell and out of all of the texts that have come through, Zeem Crawford's is the most surprising.

Are you okay?

Zeem typically sits at lunch quiet and demure. Most times he chimes in to correct someone—his IQ wouldn't allow stupidity to roam rapid for long. *Why would he text me*? We barely even talk.

I decide to respond only to him.

Hi, Zeem. I'm fine. I just had to get away for a little while.

I get a response almost immediately.

Zeem: *I'm so glad you text me back. Kyell is worried sick. I mean, literally.*

Jo: *Good.*

Zeem: *You had me worried too. I'm glad you are okay.*

Jo: *Thanks for caring, Zeem.*

Zeem: *I always have.*

Okay—that's weird. What is that supposed to mean?

Before I can decide on an answer, Mrs. Cravic comes running out of her house like it's on fire.

"Oh my God! Jozi Skies, you are going to send me to my grave!"

She runs up to me, out of breath, with gray curls flying in every direction.

"Your mom and dad are worried sick! Where did you go…," Looking me over like a certified inspector, "Are you okay?"

"I'm fine, Mrs. Cravic," I groan.

As much as I want to tell her off for touching/hugging me right now, I can't help but to think, *where do I go from here*? I made it back home, still breathing, but I still feel like jumping into that dark pool forming at the very core of me.

No one understands how miserable I feel, especially now that everyone at schools knows I'm a freak. Mrs. Cravic is talking to me, her face filled with concern, but I can't hear her.

My mind wonders to the janitor who interrupted my plan today. *Was he even real*? I see him in my mind's eye, smiling a big airy smile, saying to me, *You are going to be okay*. Then we are both floating in the air, flying up toward the sun. It's bright—so bright—but we aren't disintegrating. I lay back and bask in the sunlight.

"Jozi!"

Deep in my daydream, I failed to notice my mom and dad had pulled into the driveway. Both jump out of the car, running toward me. When they reach the step, both sit down next to me. Mick speaks first.

"Jo," he puts one arm around me, "I'm glad to see you." He kisses me on the cheek.

My mom just sits there. She looks across the street as if in a daze. "What is going on with you, Jo?"

I look over at her. "I was just thinking the same thing."

10 | Lost, On the way to Nowhere

Tonight, my parents try very hard to make everything seem normal. The twins come home, and we do our usual—sitting down at the dinner table, pretending to care about each other's day. Hazel has this look on her face like she knows something is off. She keeps glancing at my mom, then me, then back over at dad—waiting to see if one of us will break under pressure. Hannah sits quietly eating her spaghetti. At one point, I thought she might burst into tears. I'm not sure why she's always so emotional. It kind of weirds me out, so I just ignore her.

After dinner, mom follows me up to my room, but I pretend not to see her and shut my door right behind me. Of course, she knocks to come in, but I don't answer. I mean what's with these people. One minute, they want nothing to do with me and the next they won't leave me alone. I just need some quiet time. I need time to process and decompress.

Kyell hasn't tried calling or texting me since earlier today when I texted Zeem, so I guess he told him I was okay. But that shouldn't keep him from calling or texting me. I am still fuming about him telling my secret to Shelly, but my heart aches to hear his voice. Most girls desire boys for their affirmations or their good looks, but I yearn for conversations with Kyell.

Talking to him is the easiest thing in the world for me. It doesn't require me planning the next conversation starter or straining to be an active listener. It's like turning a faucet on and letting the water flow.

Kyell is like Noah from *The Notebook*. He's not the typical heart throb you read about in young adult books—he's just the opposite. He's goofy, yet sometimes very mature. He knows what he wants out of life and doesn't care what anyone thinks of him. He's smart and an amazing athlete.

Right now, he holds the record for the fastest sprinter in the state. He's very lean for a sprinter, but no one in the state is faster than him. His long legs and light frame float across the finish line like a gazelle, making him the topic of conversation during track season. If he doesn't get scholarships for academics, I am certain he will get several scholarships offers for track and field.

Kyell is in a class of his own, yet he hates to be in the spotlight. He tries his best to distract anyone from noticing his flawlessness, but it embellishes him like a royal cloak. I'm not a superficial type of girl—I mean—with my looks, what would give me the right, but Kyell is the vision of perfection. Sometimes I can tell he just jumped out of bed and didn't bother to comb his hair. But it doesn't matter, because even when his hair is shooting up in every direction, he looks good. I love his pillow-tossed look. No matter how hard he tries to look ordinary or be ordinary, it's just not possible.

Kyell is the one thing in my life that makes me want to live it and live it loud. Sometimes I wonder what it would feel like if he looked at me the way he looks at Shelly. What would it feel like to be wanted? Would I feel whole. Contemplating this thought gives me awkward images of myself being in that very moment. I shudder at the thought of my awkwardness. I probably wouldn't know how to act or even be. If I finally tell him how I truly feel, would it destroy our friendship?

I think about calling him, but my pride won't allow it. Just thinking about him betraying me sends me down a murky tunnel of anger I just can't handle right now.

How could he do this to me? How could he tell Shelly, of all people!

An image of the knife I stole from Mrs. Cravic's house comes to my mind. I imagine it in my hand again. *Just one little cut will release all the anger.* Just one cut can drown the painful questions down the drain. I can feel my blood racing through my veins.

I push the thought away and slowly lay back on the bed. I stare up at the only part of my room that isn't pink. The ceiling.

I never imagined how relaxing the dull white ceiling could be when there's so much pandemonium going on in my head. I think I will leave this part of my room as is, but the pink walls have to go—like as soon as possible. Maybe I can use my 10 day—now, nine-day—sentence to repaint my walls.

Tucking my arms behind my head, I flinch at the tinge of pain that trickles down to my fingers. I sit up quickly. I pull my sleeve up and peer down at my bruised and battered arms. The scarring is a reminder of all the times I have felt alone and unwanted.

Why would Kyell want me?

I lie back down with defeat coursing through me. My eyes begin to ache from the tears I have been desperately try-ing to hold back all day. I can't hold it in any longer. It's like an explosion has been set off, deep inside of me. I face-plant right into my pillow, holding it tightly, and let all of the pain, confusion, embarrassment, and fury pour out without any concern for who hears me.

Minutes later, I roll over on my back, heaving in big breaths of air. I know for sure, in the morning, my eyes will look like I was in a twelve-round boxing match. My mom will ask me repeatedly if I have been crying. I will tell her no, and she will proceed to make me an appointment with Dr. Brasser.

My insides recoil at the thought of the coming torture, but I decide to succumb to the beautiful silence. If she does insist on me coming out of my room tomorrow, I will just wear sunglasses.

"*What is going on with you?*" she asked.

I have no idea. I feel like someone has stuck a parachute to my back, flown me out in to the middle of nowhere, pushed me out of the plane and left me for dead. If only the massive, weird guy—I can't even remember his name—wouldn't have shown up. I would be well into a deep, peaceful sleep, never having to deal with the horrible reality I am faced with every day.

I turn over on my side and flitch at the soggy wet pillow. I turn it over to the dry side and begin sobbing out the few tears that I have left. I want them all out by tomorrow.

Tomorrow. I never thought I would see it.

11 | Saturday Morning

"Jo!"

I hear my name, but I can't move. My body feels like a wooden board.

"JO!"

A loud pounding noise sets off an excruciating throbbing in my temples. I will my eyes to stay closed.

"JO!!!"

The pounding becomes even louder. I pull my sheets over my head to block out the noise, but it only gets worse.

Fed up, I throw the covers back and sit up, my head pulsates.

"Jo! Are you in there! Are you okay!"

It's Hazel. I roll out of bed to open the door, but I stop in my tracks. The room begins to spin. I fall back down into a sitting position.

"Jo!" She nearly screams.

"Yes, Hazel! Why are you shouting? Please—please—stop," I wince, "shouting."

I still can't quite gain my balance or manage the pulsing of my heart beating in my head. I put both hands up to my temples, trying to steady myself. I feel as if I'm stuck between two pressing brick walls. I don't think I ever cried as hard as I did last night. I know I will pay for it all day today.

Trudging to the door, I let Hazel in, and she wastes no time.

"I've been calling your name forever! What is wrong with you? You didn't hear me calling you?"

"I'm fine. I'm fine. I went to sleep late and I'm still exhausted, so can you just…" I want to say, 'leave me alone,' but at least she didn't barge into my room like she normally does. I decide to be a little nicer today which shocks me.

"Give me an hour, then I'll be down."

"Okay. Mom cooked breakfast, and she said you need to eat."

"I will." I roll my eyes. Now they're trying to control when and what I'm eating, too?

"She went in to work, and dad had to go in for a few hours too, so you're stuck with us."

I groan.

"Okay, now just go away." I slowly get up from the bed and walk over to the mirror. Just as I expected, my face is all swollen from the frantic crying last night. I don't cry often; it makes me feel weak, but when I do, my face swells up like I'm allergic to emotions. The pressure behind my eyes is unbearable, my pupils are swimming in a pool of blood.

If mom could see me now. She would have called Dr. Brasser without a second thought.

For the first time in history, I am thankful for the bathroom that connects my room and the twins. Three big steps and I am in the bathroom. Quickly trying to wash the shame away. I need only to take a hot shower and this hot-air balloon I have for a face will deflate. Hopefully.

⁕⁘⁕

After showering, I feel refreshed. My vision is clearer, and walking is not a challenge anymore. Examining myself in the mirror, I notice the red blotches on my face are beginning to fade into smaller pick blush marks. I exhale. Glad I am starting to look like myself.

My bed is calling me back, but my stomach grumbles in protest. I walk over to my desk where I always keep a stash of snacks. My mouth waters at the sight of a box of chocolate chip granola bars.

As I'm opening the box, the harsh reality of yesterday and the day before sets in. The memories flood my mind, and I can't breathe. My hands shake at the thought of the blood they were covered in. Beads of sweat line my upper lip as the temperature of the room seems to rise. I take deep breaths, slowly letting them out, like Dr. Brasser instructed me.

A cool feeling fills my fingertips. My chest loosens and I exhale deeply one last time, letting out all the destructive energy. My breaths slowly become more even, and I take a big bite of my granola bar. It tastes so good, even though the box says they expired two months ago.

My cell phone buzzes from across the room. I hop up to get it. There are several new text messages. The first text is from Shelly.

I hope you are all right. Text me if you need to talk.

Rolling my eyes, I delete it. She was probably sitting right next to Kyell when she sent it. Attempting to make him think she is still a good person. He's probably stupid enough to believe it.

I tap the next message in hurry to rid my thoughts of the two of them together. It's from Kyell, sent just twenty minutes ago.

Jo, I'm coming over. I have to see you.

I drop the phone on the bed. My head spins again. Kyell. Coming. Here. He can't come here. Not today.

My phone buzzes again, and this time there's a text from Zeem.

Zeem: Hey, you doing okay?

I'm stuck. I can't text him back. Why is he texting me again? It's kind of odd he even has my number. We hardly ever talk. I get a vision of him sitting at the lunch table quietly doing his homework while everyone else rants about social media drama.

Then again, I broke someone's nose yesterday, and now the entire school knows I am unstable. Maybe he's just taking pity on me, too. I don't need his pity. I text him back.

Hi, Zeem. Thanks for checking in on me. I'm okay. Yesterday was rough.

Seconds after I hit the send button, three small dots appear. He's texting me back!

Zeem: I can imagine.

Zeem: Can you have company?

My stomach turns a flip as if I just jumped off the highest diving board. Then, I hear the door-bell. *Kyell.*

Jo: Probably not. Why?

Zeem: I just thought you might want some company.

The twins' high-pitched laughter drifts upstairs. Kyell is definitely here. They only laugh like that when he's around. He just has that effect on people.

Jo: Maybe when my incarceration is over?

I feel guilty for blowing him off. He seems to be genuine and God knows I need those kinds of people in my life.

Zeem: That's fine. I'll wait.

I don't know how to respond to that, so I don't. I just stare down at the words. *I'll wait.* A powerful knock rattles the door of my bedroom. Zeem texts again.

Zeem: I guess I'll see you in ten days then?

Jo: I guess so.

Zeem: Cool.

I sit my phone down to get a quick glimpse of myself in the mirror. My eyes are still swollen, and my face needs another hour before it's back to normal.

"Jo?"

Kyell's voice flows through the door, intoxicating me and pushing my cares out of the window.

Patting a few stray hairs down, I rush over to open the door. He steps across the threshold and grabs me before I can even get a good look at him.

"Oh, Jo. I'm so glad you are okay."

I embrace him, his arms wrapped around me, and I finally feel safe. Wanted. Seen. I lean in with my entire body—holding on-to him like he's my lifeline.

When he finally releases me, he looks down at me with those sharp goofy eyes. This is the look he gives me when he's about to say something stupid.

"I didn't know you were an MMA fighter." He nudges me as he walks by, throwing out air jabs, then flops down on the edge of my bed.

A smile doesn't form, and I don't allow the slightest giggle to escape my mouth. I am still so mad at him I could scream. But I don't. I'm just happy he's here. But I can't let him off the hook so easily. I have to know why he would do something so awful. But, instead, I calmly walk over to the window.

"You know I'm suspended, which probably means I am grounded too."

"I know. I just wanted to stop by to say I'm sorry—to your face."

I hear footsteps coming toward me, then his warmth reaches my back. He places his hands on my shoulders, a gesture that makes me want to forgive him right here—right now.

"I'm sorry, Jo."

There are times I long to be close to him—to be close enough to him to feel his energy surge through me. Today, I want him to know how much he has hurt me. He needs to experience the same ache I feel inside. But my love for him contends with my anger. I want to kiss him just as much as I want to punch him.

I step away, trying to contain both emotions so they don't bubble over and make a gigantic mess of things.

He stares at me, then drops his arms. "I. I don't know what else to do Jo. There's no way I can take back what I did. If I could God knows I would."

"Kyell, you had no right telling Shelly anything about me!" I yell it out so loud I startle myself and him.

"In my defense, Jo, we are all friends. You two used to be so close. I thought she needed to know. So, we both could keep an eye on you."

My fists clench and my teeth grind. I take a step closer towards him.

"Keep an eye on me! What do I look like…"

Kyell's eyes grow big. I realize he has never seen me this angry. I don't think I have ever revealed myself in this way to anyone.

Well, there was that time I broke someone's nose.

I take several deep breaths to calm down. My blood runs evenly again after the third breath.

"We are not close. We barely even talk. I can't believe you haven't noticed that. Oh wait, how could you? You're too busy fawning over her every move."

I go back to looking out the window, ashamed I even said anything about how he acts around her and embarrassed I allowed my jealous thoughts to become spoken words.

He doesn't move. I can hear his steady breathing just a few feet away.

"Jozi, I can't say that you're wrong. I hadn't noticed."

"Go figure," I mutter, not moving my gaze from the front driveway. I think there's another crack that wasn't there before.

"I—I just can't seem to shake what I feel for her. She's always giving me this look, like she knows how I feel. And sometimes I think she feels the same way. Maybe it's lust, but to me—I think its love. I think I'm in love with her, Jo."

Tears form behind my eyes and my heart rips straight down the middle. Every muscle in my body tenses up. I want to crumble to the floor like a decrepit building, but I don't. I stand firm.

"Kyell," my voice cracks at the sound of his name, "please leave."

"Jozi, I didn't mean to hurt you. I just wanted to help. I thought…"

Tears escape my eyes like rapid rain drops. I leave the window and gently guide him to my bedroom door.

"Jo, I thought she could help—hey Jo. You're crying?"

"I am crying, dummy, because *I* love you."

He stares at me from the hallway. He is motionless. His sharp black eyes trained on me. I close the door of my room. I close the door on this love, this friendship, this chapter.

12 | Dr. Brasser

Today is the first official day of my suspension. Since Saturday, I haven't been out of my room much, and I haven't eaten anything since the granola bar. I tried hard to bounce back after Kyell left. He tried knocking and calling out to me, but I guess the shock of what I said took its toll. Ignoring him has been more difficult than anything I have ever experienced. That night, after I slept through the entire day, my phone buzzed from underneath my pillow at least one hundred times. After waking up from a nightmare at three in the morning, I got the nerve to read a few texts from him.

I know you are mad at me. Hopefully, you will get over it like you've done so many times before. You are one of my best friends, Jo.

Friend. The word sends me into a place of numbness. He would ignore the most obvious. *Why did you tell him? You are the stupidest, most pathetic person on the planet, Jozi Skies.*

I stared down at the text for hours that night, reading it repeatedly, letting the words bounce around in my head and then in my heart until I fell off to sleep.

My mom came in several times on Sunday. I remember little of what she said. She hugged me gently and left a sandwich and a coke on my nightstand. Mick also came in to check on me. He mentioned Kyell, and for a moment, I came back down to earth.

"I spoke to Kyell this evening," Mick said. "I told him it was okay if he stopped by for a little while."

I lost it. "NO, it is not!" Again, I had to calm down with the breathing techniques. Mick didn't protest, and Kyell never came, so I guess he listened.

Mick seems to be the only person other than Mrs. Cravic who has a clue about how I feel for Kyell, but he has never mentioned it.

This morning, my mom made me get dressed. I stumbled around for an hour trying to will myself into the shower. 1. Because I hate doing what she tells me to do and 2. I know what today is. I have to make my first visit to Dr. Brasser. I suck it up and do what is inevitable.

The back of my throat feels like someone has poured sawdust in it. I open my mouth to let the water run in. The drops of water feel refreshing and I feel my body absorbing every drop.

By some miracle, I make it out to the car where I get to listen to my mom as she drones on about eating, drinking, and death.

"Jo, are you trying to kill yourself by dehydration, or starvation?"

That wouldn't be a bad idea, but it takes three days to die from dehydration, and starvation would be a much longer and painful death.

"You will spend an hour with Dr. Brasser," my mom rambles on. "Maybe she can help you get out of this funk you're in."

I say nothing. I think I can stomach Dr. Brasser for an hour. Her tools have helped me to stay calm enough to escape a homicide.

I stare out the window; the sunshine peering through the trees snagging my attention. When I was in middle school, I loved venturing off to faraway places and writing fantasy stories.

Once I wrote a short story about a girl who lived in Seattle. She was born in Fairbanks, Alaska, where daylight lasts for 24 hours during some of the summer months of the year and where some people cover their windows with aluminum foil to sleep. Her parents named her Sunni because she was born during the summer solstice.

When she was five years old, they moved to Washington. Even though she was young, she knew she did not want to move. She became someone else inside and changed completely. After two months of gloomy, cloud-filled skies, Sunni slept. She slept, and she slept, and she slept. Her parents couldn't figure out how to wake her. Then, one day, the sun came up longer than it had in the last two months, and Sunni woke up. This is when they realized that she could only wake up when the sun was out. Her parents figured out a way to keep her awake as long as they could. They replaced all the light bulbs in her room with a new technology that caused the same UV rays the sun would cast. Sunni didn't like it, so she continued to sleep until she grew old. One day she woke up and no one was there. I ended it like that. Content on the unhappy ending.

Now, I wish I was Sunni. I guess, back then, I created the story as the perfect Utopia for me. Sleep. Sunshine. Parents who disappear after seemly one night of sleep. How can you go wrong with a life like that?

The weird metal ball contraption sitting on Dr. Brasser's desk is mesmerizing. I could sit here all day just watching these balls clash into each other, but I know it's only a matter of minutes before the interrogation begins.

Isn't it funny? The balls are more therapeutic than the lady with the PH.D.

I scan the bookshelf standing against the wall next to me. A book called, "It's All in Your Imagination," stands out to me. I hear that more than I would care to admit. My imagination has always been vast.

The door behind me shuts, then Dr. Brasser strides past me and takes a seat at her desk. Thank God her desk is right in front of a large window, so I have something to distract me from looking at her small, dull face. She's a petite woman. Her tiny frame fits her oval face, but her black plastic glasses drown her face, and gives her this childish, entirely ridiculous, impossible-to take seriously, look. She is plain, to say the least.

Her hair is always the same, straight part down the middle and pulled back into a doughnut. Watching her is like watching ice melt. Boring. No wonder she doesn't wear a ring. Who would marry her?

She grabs her notebook, a thin silver pen, and walks over to the stereotypical "therapeutic" lawn chair.

"Okay, Jozi. Are you ready?"

"Eh, not quite." I get up from my comfortably warm spot. I don't want to prolong this hour—not even one second.

When I move across the room, I am suddenly aware of my intense hunger. My stomach feels like it has just possibly caved in on itself. It growls—loudly, begging for food. Dr. Brasser stares at me in silent questions.

She takes her index finger and forces her glasses up to their proper position.

"Would you like some crackers? I have some in my drawer." She doesn't wait for my response, but pivots to her desk drawer and retrieves a white and yellow box. "They are made of flaxseeds and oats. They're so yummy." She giggles. And they're gluten-free!"

Anything would taste good at this point.

She hands the box to me. I take them without protest.

"Thank you." Then, I lay back in the stupid leather chair.

"Sure." She picks up her pen and notebook once more. "So, your mom has caught me up on everything that has happened in the past four days. Let's start from the beginning. Thursday, what made you so upset in class that day?"

Stuffing a few crackers in my mouth, I chew and pretend I'm thinking hard. When I finish with that mouthful, I put two more crackers in and begin chewing.

Dr. Brasser exhales deeply. "You know, this session will go a lot smoother if you just cooperate. Besides, if you keep this up, I may have to see you Wednesday *and* Friday."

I sit up to get a sip of water. I clear my throat and silently agree to answer her questions. As long as I don't have to come back two more times this week.

"Rowan told everyone that I cut myself. Well, she didn't say it like that. It was more like, 'Show everyone how you fileted your arms.'"

"I see." She keeps her head down. Fixated on the notes she's scribbling in that dumb notebook of hers.

She glances up at me. "So, how did you relieve your anger this time?"

I put my index figure up to my temple and tap a few times like I have to think about it for a few seconds.

"Uh, I think I—I punched her in her nose. And broke it. Don't you already know this!"

"So, you didn't think to try the calming methods we talked about the last time you were here?"

"Uh," I tap my temple again, "No—those calming methods didn't cross my mind with a classroom full of my peers staring at me like some psycho!"

"I see."

I roll my eyes at that condescending phrase. *No, you don't see. You are basically blind—even with those hideous glasses fixed to your face.*

"Do you regret what you did?"

I scowl at the thought of Rowan's face. "Nope. She deserved it and I would do it all over again."

Several minutes pass, with Dr. Brasser busily writing God-knows-what on her legal pad. Frustrated, I blow loudly into the air.

"Okay, Jozi," She looks up at me. "Where were you on Friday, the day after they suspended you? Your parents couldn't find you for at least two hours."

I don't reply. This time I keep my hands clasped together on top of my abdomen. She taps the thin silver pen on her notebook. The tapping begins to annoy me, and I adjust myself in the chair.

"Jozi? Where did you go after you left Mrs. Cravic's house?"

"Why does it matter?" I snap at her. "I'm here now. I didn't go off and kill myself. And besides, isn't this supposed to be a therapy session, not an interrogation?"

Dr. Brasser speaks in a slow melodic voice, I guess to calm me, but it only makes me feel even more unstable. That's how you talk to someone who is unstable.

"Yes, I know. I'm so glad you are here. Safe and sound." She lets those last two words drift up into the air. "But in order to help you get past all of this you have to be willing to state the facts. Tell me where you went."

I concede, remembering the time. "I went to Clear View."

"And why did you go there?"

I close my eyes, seeing myself sitting in the stall once again. "To get revenge."

"And how were you going to get revenge, Jozi?"

I pause—keeping my eyes closed. If I tell her the truth—the shameful truth—she will tell my parents, and they might just send me away.

So, I lie.

"I would tell all of Rowan's secrets by writing them on the bathroom walls."

"So, did you?"

"No. Someone stopped me."

I giggle at the memory of the strange person I met that day. His full image hovers right beneath the back of my eyelids: cool, spiked auburn hair, calming blue eyes, and a firm stance.

His face is just as ageless and its glowing like the sun on a cool spring day. I grin as he smiles right back at me.

"Who stopped you, Jozi? Was it another student?"

"No, it was..." I can't quite remember his name. "He told me..."

There's a whisper in my ear, a tickle, and I jolt forward into a sitting position.

"ADAR. H—his name is Adar."

Dr. Brasser looks up from her notebook. "Are you okay?"

My eyes scan the room. Nothing.

Slowly, I lay back again, "Yes. I'm fine."

She will freak out if I tell her, so—I tell her.

"His name's Adar. At first, I thought he was the new janitor, but he looks too young to be a janitor. Usually the janitors at Clear View look to be uncles or grandpas. Nah, I thought, he can't be. And technically, he really didn't say that he was, when I asked him. He said he cleans things up, but it seemed like he diverted my question. Then, when I ran to the door, after he left, there was no trace of him. I mean, it was like he had disappeared. I'm not..."

"Wait. Just slow down, Jozi. I'm not following. There was a strange man in the girl's bathroom that you have never seen around the school before?"

"Yes. He was very kind and..."

"Wait. Please. What was he wearing?"

Dr. Brasser writes on a fresh piece of notebook paper, wearing a very critical expression.

I grin and keep talking. "He was wearing a pair of jeans, with rips at the knee and a white t-shirt. And sandals. Really comfortable-looking sandals."

"Wow, Jozi. You should have told someone about this strange man. What if—"

"Whatever, he was harmless. Besides, I didn't want anyone to know I showed up there and I was suspended—which is why you have to keep this between us—patient confidentiality, remember?"

She pauses. "Yeah, but the agreement is between your parents and me. You are a minor."

I sit up again. "Please, Dr. Brasser. Please don't tell them I went to the school. They will want to know why. I regret it.

I really do. And if you do this for me, I will know I can trust you—that I can tell you anything."

She drops the pen on top of the notebook and stares at me. Maybe this reversed psychology will work. Beat her at her own game.

"Okay," she finally says. She tears out the new set of notes she started and balls them up. "You can trust me, Jozi. I am here for you."

"Good." I lean back into the chair again as she picks up her pen once more. "Anyway, I told you, he's harmless. I actually think he's an angel. My guardian angel."

"And why do you think that?" Her scribbling pen hesitates, and she looks up, crocking an eyebrow.

"Because he had wings."

"What?!"

The sound of that pen dropping to the notepad is priceless.

13 | Crazy?

After Dr. Brasser calmed down, she told me that Adar is a figment of my imagination. She matter-of-factly explained that many people suffering from severe depression and/or anxiety can tend to create worlds, characters, and situations that are not real. I remembered the book, *It's All in Your Imagination,* and just listened as she destroyed the image of Adar—piece by piece.

I leave her office feeling unsettled. Confused, even. Isn't that an oxymoron? To leave therapy feeling even more confused.

Maybe I am crazy.

I open the passenger door of my mom's Volkswagen, replaying Dr. Brasser's words—over and over again in my head. My instincts tell me someone is watching me. I scan my environment and glimpse a tall, slender man across the street. He quickly looks away and begins walking.

Was he staring at me?

The white shirt he's wearing provokes me to tiptoe to see over the roof of the car to get a better look at his face—well, now, the back of his head.

It can't be.

My mom finally catches up with me after having her routine debriefing with Dr. Brasser. It's just another way to invade my privacy. She blocks my view as she opens her door. Annoyed, I duck my head around her, beckoning her to get into the car quicker, but she notices my distraction and tries to set eyes on what I'm looking at.

"What are you so focused on?" She asks, turning around to see.

"Mom!" I yell in frustration.

"What?" She looks around, still obstructing my view. "What is it?"

"The guy across the street. Please move."

By the time she turns back to me, he's gone.

"I don't see anyone, Jo."

"Ugh," I roll my eyes and get in the car, mumbling under my breath. "Why can't you just mind your own business?"

"What?" She asks, completely clueless.

I guess it is all in my imagination.

❦

It's Tuesday, just days before I'm destined to return to hell and the days can't move any faster. I finished the work Kyell dropped off to Mick an hour ago and there's still several hours before the twins get home. I want today to go by fast because I actually hate being home alone, but I also want it to go by slowly because I am not looking forward to getting back to school anytime soon.

Sitting home alone is terrifying when you think you're going crazy.

Mrs. Cravic came over to make me breakfast this morning, but, of course, it's her way of keeping an eye on me. Even though I despise being watched, it is better than being in an empty house right now.

I go downstairs to watch a little T.V. to calm my nerves. I feel with every move I make someone is moving right along with me. I dash to the couch, taking a quick scan of the living room.

Nope. No one here but me.

My chest deflates. I blow out the subtle fear of the unknown.

Remote in hand, I flip through the channels. Nothing good is ever on this early in the morning. Early Bird TV is what I call it: game shows, court shows, and soap operas. A few music videos and a cartoon episode catch my attention, but not for long. Then I see it. In big white letters. ANGELS. In all caps, cast across the screen. I flip back three channels, trying to find the image I just saw. Once there, the letters fade into a studio audience backdrop. An ominous instrumental plays as a man with snow white hair walks out to center stage.

"Hello, Bill Alston here. Welcome to my universe, where it's naturally, SUPERNATURAL!"

My sixth sense tells me to flip back to the cartoon episode, but I can't. I am transfixed.

"My guest today is here to share her encounters with celestial beings we like to call, ANGELS."

This can't be happening.

I look around because, again, a cool draft of air fills the room. I shiver. And again, I realize it's just me. Alone. There's no one here but me, but I can't help but think of Adar's words, and the presence I have felt with me since that day in the bathroom. I focus on the man on T.V. He's an old and slender man, with a grandpa feel. Desperate for clarity, I run over to mom's desk to grab a pen and a piece of paper.

A fair-skinned, well put together woman walks out on stage dressed in a flowing royal blue dress.

"There are five things you need to know about angels. These may seem simple and ordinary, but it's important to know and remember…"

I write them down:

1). *Usually accompanied with light.*
2). *Not all angels have wings-most angels that will visit earth do not have wings.*
3). *They are messengers of God-here to share what God wants to say to you.*
4). *They can appear as human beings here on earth.*
5). *And 90% of angel encounters are coincidental*

I stop writing.

I read what I have written. Everything checks off. Light. No wings. I'm not sure about the messenger of God part, but he looked normal to me, except for his extraordinary eyes. And it was coincidental for him to be there—in the girl's bathroom—right when I was about to…

She interrupts my thoughts with a story.

"My first encounter with an Angel was on a hike with a few friends. We decided to challenge our bodies and hike a massive mountain just a few miles from the Mexican border. I was contemplating thoughts of divorcing my husband at the time and needed some time away from the house and the kids.

We reached the top with little to no struggle. It felt great to conquer the mountain, but as I had hoped, I hadn't discovered the courage I needed to conquer my marriage.

On the way down, I remember being so blinded by the sun that I began to stumble. No matter how I squinted, or shielded my eyes, the sun wasn't letting up. I could hear my friends voices a few feet in front of me, so I sauntered along confidently. Suddenly, I felt myself slam into something or should I say someone.

It was a lady that appeared to be around 50 to 60 years of age, coming *up* the mountain. Afraid that I startled her, I immediately apologize and begin checking to see if she was okay.

I remember it as if it just happened. She wore glasses and dressed in all khaki: a khaki safari hat, and Khaki button up shirt, shorts and sandals. Of all things to wear on a mountain. Sandals!"

I laugh, she laughs, and the old guy, Bill, does, too.

Sandals? Adar and his comfy looking sandals bring a smile to my face.

"By this time my friends had stopped and turned back to see who I was speaking to. They looked at each other, confused. Later they would tell me they never remembered the lady passing them.

Bill was mystified. "What did she say?"

"She said, 'Oh, Hi!'"

I was taken aback, but I still replied quickly with a 'Hi.' Suddenly, a calm washed over me. This was something I still can't explain. I was simply calm. The next few moments wouldn't seem weird or even scary until after the encounter, but I remember our conversation very well.

First, she asked me my name. Before I could answer she said, 'Wait, it's quite a unique name?'

'Yes.' I replied without missing a beat.'"

"Whoa," Bill interrupts her. "So you are telling me the women just stops you in your tracks and asks your name? Just like that?"

"Yes. Like I said, I don't think of it as strange at this point. I just engage. I tell her my name, but as I do this, she sounds out the first syllable *for* me.

"Oh my, as if she already knew your name?"

"Yes, when I tell her she shakes her head in recognition and repeats it."

'Sssantita. What a beautiful name. Do you know what it means?' She asks me.

"Because my name is so unique, no one ever pronounces it right the first time. Dumbfounded, I tell her, 'Yes, it means Saint.' She nods in approval, then continues up the mountain. When she passes me, I turn around to take another look at her—to exclaim, once again, that I am sorry for bumping into her. She turns around to say, 'No worries. And don't worry about anything, Santita, you will make it safely. You just can't give up.'

Looking back toward my friends, who all are still wearing a confused scowl on their faces, I ponder what she could mean. Suddenly, just as soon as I got a glimpse of their faces, it hit me. I knew exactly what she was talking about. I turned back quickly, but she was gone."

"So, what did you do…" Bill asks. "…after you went home?"

"I stayed with my husband and we have been going strong ever since."

I take in the story. Feeling calmer than I have all day and tired. Really tired.

My encounter was more traumatic than hers. I mean, Adar appeared in the girl's bathroom with jeans and a t-shirt on. He didn't look like an angel—more like a t-shirt model.

Because I'm just not the scary type.

The hair on my neck stands to attention. I freeze in a crouched position. Willing myself not to turn around—not to even breath. Staring at the screen in front of me, one word stands out. *Guardian.* I can't take my eyes off that word. Guardian. Guardian. Guardian, I repeat it to myself over and over again.

Yep, that's me—makes me sound official.

I jump at the voice that sounds a little closer this time. For a split second, I get up the nerve to do what my mind keeps telling me not to do. I turn around.

No one. There's no one.

I turn back around, slowly, looking at the same words again.

Okay, I will reveal myself only if you promise not to faint or die... or anything.

The voice sounds lively, and familiar which puts me at ease. My heart calms and my breathing follows. Peering over my shoulder, I still see no one.

Dr. Brasser is probably right about me. It's all in my imagination. This quite frankly justifies everybody at school calling me looney. Hearing voices. Looking for angels. Trying to glimpse something that isn't there. I settle within myself to just ignore what I'm hearing.

I said, I will show myself to you if you promise to chill-OUT.

Ignoring the voice, I turn off the T.V. To put my mind on something else; I go into my mom's office and I google, "famous libraries." Yeah, that's interesting stuff. Libraries make any situation brighter.

Scrolling through the list, I stop on the beautiful five story, George Peabody Library in Baltimore, Maryland. I tried planning to see it the last time I visited Grandma Ellis, but mom allowed the twins to steer her in another direction.

Psst.

My fingers stall over the mouse. I am motionless for several seconds, then I resume my failing attempt to ignore this, in my estimation, paranormal activity.

It's hard to ignore the sounds I'm hearing, but the tap on my shoulder is unbearable. I keep my eyes on the screen, but the second tap isn't letting up. I slowly cock my head to peer over my shoulder. And as sure as the sky is blue, there *is* someone standing over me, tapping me on my shoulder.

This time I turn with super precision to catch the culprit. Standing not even three feet away from me is the same man I met in the girl's bathroom the other day.

With all the breath I can muster, I shirk, "Adar!"

He jumps back a bit, giving me some space. The look on his face is a cross between frightened and concerned.

I'm inhaling in heaves. My hands are shaking uncontrollably, but I keep my eyes set on him. His sandals actually.

Okay, just chill out. I'm sorry. I thought you were calm.

Breathlessly, I manage to get out, "Well, obviously… I'm… not calm!"

Okay…Okay… you're right. You're not. I'm sorry. I'm so sorry.

He looks around nervously, like he's trying to figure out what to do. He reaches out to touch my head. His touch calms me immediately.

You okay now? You need some water?

"No," looking down at the floor. I feel a sense of euphoria. Like my brain has been wiped clean of every negative memory and thought and filled with thoughts of unicorns, cotton candy and rainbows.

"How did you do that? What did you do to me?"

He smiles with triumph. Oh it's just something I picked up from Shalom Himself.

"Who?"

You never heard of Him?

He asks this with anticipation for an immediate answer, but he comprehends the blank stare and continues.

Well, Peace. I just gave you a little peace. A peace that is difficult to understand, but so easy to accept. With His permission, of course.

He leans against the wall in relief and slowly slides down into a sitting position.

When he's finally to me eye level, I look him over. I guess this peace thing is working because I can look at him without diverting my eyes and I don't feel weird.

Wow. He looks so young.

His hair is shooting off in every direction, which gives him this boyish look. The shadow of facial hair tells me that maybe he's in his late twenties—early thirties. He shoots a sly smirk in my direction. It's odd, I think he can hear my thoughts. Then he confirms.

I am a rookie at this kind of thing, but I am definitely not young.

"Why are you here? How are you here?" I finally ask— surprised that I can even speak, let alone ask questions.

I'm here because I would like to show you something.

He says this with an alluring smile.

And if you promise not to start calling yourself crazy again I'll tell you how I got here?

I lean forward in the chair tucking my hands under my legs, intrigued. "Sure."

We travel by the speed of light.

"We?"

Angels! I'm your guardian angel, Jozi. Here to serve and protect.

With the same charming smile, he salutes me like a soldier in my brigade.

14 | Grandma Ellis

Cast into another dimension like a sonic boom, I come to myself while standing in Grandma Ellis's bedroom. She's kneeling down on the floor. The lights are off, but the low beams of sunlight escaping from behind the curtains give the room an orange glow. It's evening. Grandma Ellis should just have finished eating dinner.

I draw in a deep breath, savoring the smells of cinnamon and sugar. She loves the scent and always keeps a full stock of cinnamon and sugar candles in her closet. I'd forgotten the smell. It's been so long.

In the corner of the room, I notice a flickering mirage. The sunlight from the window reflects off it making it difficult to make out the image. I try to focus my eyes, but I'm pushed forward by a voice.

Walk closer.

Reluctantly, I obey.

Slow and steady, I inch closer to her. She doesn't move. She doesn't even realize I am here. Her mouth is moving, but I can't hear anything. A cool breeze blows right behind me.

I look over my shoulder and there *he* is. Adar. The once blurry image is now perfectly clear

He stands near the door. Suddenly, I feel like someone has just turned up the volume on a radio station. In loud surround sound, I hear a stream of cries.

Sobbing. Completely overcome. Grandma Ellis cries out even louder. I cross my arms over my chest to keep myself from putting my arms around her.

She raises her head from the floor.

"Oh God! Take care of my Jozi!" She collapses back onto the floor.

Somehow, I can feel her pain. The emptiness inside of me aches and I hug my stomach. Alarmed at a tickle on my cheek, I quickly wipe tears away.

"Send your angels to protect her and keep her in all of her ways. Oh God, wrap your loving arms around her! Don't let her go. Please—please, don't let her go!"

I break down. I drop to my knees beside her. "I'm right here, Grandma. I'm right here."

She can't hear you, Jozi. Adar says softly.

I'm suddenly frightened. This all seems so real. But, it can't be.

This is what your Grandma Ellis was doing the day you ran away from Mrs. Cravic's house. Your mom couldn't find you, so she called the only person that could calm her. Grandma Ellis went straight to prayer. She's the reason I showed up. The fervent prayer of the righteous can get a lot done here on earth.

I look up at him, speechless. I get up from the floor and the sound of Grandma's cries dial down again. She continues to rock, back and forth, sending prayers up—for me.

Wiping tears from my eyes, I catch my breath enough to mumble out, "I'm still so mad at her. She is the reason I feel like I am living in a prison. If she wouldn't have told…"

If she wouldn't have told your mom you were cutting yourself, you would not be here right now. She told because she loves you.

I look up at him, then back over at Grandma Ellis. "What if that's what I want? What if I want to die?"

I jolt up into a sitting position. My face is drenched in tears.

I am back in my living room. The T.V. is still on and there's a different old guy on the screen. In the top right corner, I see the words "GTV"

I look around, franticly. "Grandma?"

"Grandma!" There's no answer.

⁕⁂⁕

When I regain a sense of awareness, the questions begin to flow.

What just happened?

That janitor was here.

Was I hallucinating? Was it real? Or was I just having a weird dream?

I search feverishly for a good show to watch—hoping to rid the room of the clouding creepiness in the air.

The clock says the twins should be here by now. I glance over my shoulder, out the window toward the curb.

Still no sign of them.

Moments later, I hear the loud exhaust of the bus. I look out of the window once more, an exhale escapes me. I've never been so relieved to see them. As the twins get off the bus I run to meet them in the driveway. Hannah's face is flushed. She's been crying, again.

Why does she insist on crying in front of everybody? I imagine her cowering in her bus window. I don't want everyone thinking she's a cry baby—which she is.

Hazel wraps her arm around her.

Words escape me.

Grandma Ellis. I have to call her, but first, I have to find out what's going on with Hannah. Then, after all of that, I think I need to pay Dr. Brasser another visit. Today, has been…a day.

15 | Hannah

My twin sisters—well, I wish I could say I enjoy them, but I don't. As annoying as they may be, I still can't stand to see them cry.

Hannah walks numbly to the adjourning loveseat as if she doesn't see me. I walk into the kitchen to find Hazel, I guess getting them some snacks.

"What's wrong with Hannah, today?"

Hazel ignores me too and busies herself with her task.

I look back over at Hannah who is now sitting down on the couch, staring at the blank television.

"What's up?" I plop down next to her.

Hazel walks over with two glasses of orange juice and hands one to Hannah. She acts so grown up. The way she speaks—tone and vernacular—are way too much for me to handle sometimes.

She's only eleven.

She likes to wear her hair like mine, drawn back in a high ponytail. Their hair is dark brown like my mom's, but their curls are tight and thick like mine. Mom has always insisted they be placed in the same class. They wear different-colored ribbons, to make it easy on their teachers, but I'm sure they can easily tell them apart.

Hazel will talk you under a rock and Hannah you barely realize is in the room. To me, Hazel's features are sharper than Hannah's. Her bone structure is more defined, while Hannah has a rounder face. Her entire body has gotten rounder in the past few months, but she isn't fat, yet. At times, I can tell she is a little self-conscious about it. She's constantly looking at the nutrition facts on everything, and she checks her weight before bed every night. I hear her getting on the scale when she thinks Hazel and I are asleep.

When I tried to explain to her it is best to check her weight in the morning instead of at night, she looked at me like I called her a bad name and stormed out of the bathroom. I just laughed. I have enough troubles of my own. I can't be bothered about her issues with her weight.

As usual, Hazel speaks up first.

"Hannah and I couldn't sit together on the bus today and I guess something happened. She hasn't told me yet because you rudely interrupted."

"I ignore Hazel and push Hannah's big curly strands of hair back from her face.

"What's wrong Hannah?"

She doesn't say anything. Hazel sits next to her and takes a sip of her orange juice.

"She's not going to tell me if you are sitting here. Why don't you go back to your room? I will prepare dinner tonight."

I roll my eyes, trying very hard not to go off on Hazel. I am losing patience with both of them.

"Hannah, tell me why you were crying." I ask more firmly.

Hannah flinches. It's odd, they know I don't play around when I'm asking them something and they're not answering. Hazel is snappy and loves to play the boss, but she knows who really runs the show until mom or dad gets home.

"Why are you so jumpy, Hannah?"

She doesn't answer. She keeps her eyes trained on the blank television.

"Hannah, if you don't tell me what's going on with you right now, I am going to—"

"What? She glares at me. "What are *you* going to do? You don't care, so stop trying to act like how I feel matters to you! All you care about is yourself!"

She shoots up from the couch and runs up the stairs. I look over at Hazel who is slowly sipping her orange juice.

I lean back in the couch and exhale loudly, "Can you please tell me what that was all about?"

"I think she had a bad day at school. The reason we couldn't sit together on the bus is because she got on late."

"Why?"

"I don't know. She is usually waiting for me at the end of the hallway, but today she wasn't there. I waited for her for a little while. Eventually, I left. I figured maybe she forgot something in class and had to go back."

"So, do you think something happened on the bus or at school?"

"I'm not sure."

"Well, can you find out and then come tell me?"

Hazel rolls her eyes. "Now is not a good time. Let's give her some time alone. Then, I'll go up and talk to her."

My foot begins to do a slow and steady tap against the floor, annoyed with yet another grown up gesture from Hazel. I have to admit, she does have a good point. In a way they both remind me of myself.

"Okay. I'll make dinner while you figure it out."

She picks up her glass of orange juice and takes a sip, "Sure."

16 | Zeem

Today hasn't been all that bad. I made it through an entire morning without feeling lost. Dr. Brasser would be proud. My little encounter with Adar this morning seems distant and somewhat of a vague dream, although the feeling I am not alone has been a glaring overcast for days now. I can no longer ignore it.

It's five o'clock now and I realize I have not thought about Kyell all day, well almost. The vision, dream, or whatever it was has kept my mind occupied. Unlike any other time before, thinking about Kyell leads to unwanted memories and thoughts. For one—School.

Eight more days.

Hazel is upstairs, hopefully, getting to the bottom of why Hannah is always upset. This gives me time to focus my thoughts on something else. Dinner.

I decide to prepare something simple and something everyone will like—tacos. The only tedious thing about making tacos is cutting up the tomatoes. My knife skills aren't all that great and cutting tomatoes into small bite-sized pieces isn't easy.

After I drain the oil from the ground beef and add the taco seasoning, I start on the daunting tomatoes. As soon as I make the second oozing cut, my phone buzzes. A part of me hopes it's Kyell. Another part of me hopes it's Grandma Ellis. Now, I miss her more than ever.

I grab the dish towel hanging on the sink and wipe my wet slimy fingers before picking up the phone. It's Zeem.

How was your day?

I am asked that question every day, but for some reason, this time, its different. It's genuine. Like he really wants to know.

I don't text him back. I just go back to cutting.

That nagging voice in my head begins to rattle off again. *Why is he texting me so much lately? Maybe Kyell put him up to it?* I scowl. *No, Kyell has enough to keep him busy. He's probably relieved to not have to worry about pitiful little me.*

Zeem. I have thought of him more in the past few days than I have in the past six years. Zeem is one of Kyell's closest friends. They have known each other their whole lives. Since they were in elementary school they have been involved in track and field together. They met one summer during track club. Since their dad's work for the same government contractor, it made it easy for the entire family to connect.

Zeem holds the second fastest time in the mile. Kyell holds first. Kyell lives and breathes track while Zeem coasts through anything academic. I guess you can say Zeem is good at pretty much everything, too. But he has no problem giving Kyell recognition for being more athletic. Zeem is shorter than Kyell but has the physique of an Olympic sprinter—muscular and powerful. Kyell's slender body makes him more agile and light on his feet, making him the fastest at every event.

No one knows how I feel about Kyell, except maybe Grandma Ellis. I don't think Zeem knows, but the way he stares into my soul sometimes, he might. But, if he did, I don't think he would be sending me these awkward texts.

I want to text him back, but I have no idea what to say. A part of me feels like he is flirting, but another part of me says, maybe he's just trying to be nice.

I scrape the knife across the cutting board, raking all the diced tomatoes into a small glass bowl. Wiping my hands once again, I pick up my phone.

Jo: It was uneventful to say the least. How was yours?

Zeem: It was alright. Practice was rough? Coach Boyd, wasn't holding back today. My entire body is in pain.

Jo: Someone must of have been late? LoL!

Zeem: No, he just loves to see us suffer, especially the upper classman. He wants to strike fear into the freshman and sophomores so he's using us as guinea pigs

Jo: I see.

He doesn't text back. I wait. Nothing. I text again.

Jo: I dread going back to school, Zeem.

Zeem: I know. Just know... I'm here for you. And... you also have Ky.

Butterflies dance in my stomach, but I'm not sure if it's because of what he said about Ky—or what he said about himself.

Jo: I guess.

Zeem: I really miss seeing your face, Jo. School isn't the same without you.

Jo: I will see you soon.

Zeem: You promise?

I try to shake the feeling, but the butterflies are persistent. They *are* dancing for him. Awkward.

Jo: I promise.

17 | Mick

Just as Hazel comes down the stairs, Mick pushes open the front door. It's not often he gets home before mom. Typically, he gets in right after we begin eating dinner. He's about an hour early.

Hazel runs into his arms and he lifts her up from the ground, as if she was a feather. She giggles like a little girl. I recoil at the façade she wears around Mick and mom.

Mick smiles down at her as he gently lowers her to the floor.

"I better pick you up as much as I can. Pretty soon you'll be too big."

He used to say that to me all the time. Now, when I hear him saying that to the twins my insides tighten—and I feel as though I've lost him. Before they came along life was so much easier with him.

He walks over to me and kisses my cheek. "Isn't that right, Jo?"

"Yeah. If he's too old to pick me up now, Hazel, imagine how old he'll be when you are 16."

And just like that I am swept off my feet and spinning around in Mick's arms. I squeal with surprise. Mick laughs loudly, comes to a slow spin and gently lowers my legs. I hop down out of his arms, still laughing. Mick grins, staring me right in my eyes, breathless.

"It's been a while since I've done that," he says.

Small little lines have formed under his eyes. Mick's handsome. He used to look just like Justin Timberlake to me. Now he looks like an older version of him. At this moment, I realize how much time has gone by since I looked at him and truly *saw* him.

It was probably the last time he truly saw me. He's been way too busy to notice me.

"Yeah, because you're getting old."

"And don't I know it!" He slumps over even more, putting one hand on his back, and playfully limps to the kitchen table.

Hazels skips over and sits down on his lap.

"Where's Hannah?" He asks.

"Oh, she's just getting washed up for dinner," Hazel replies.

Hazel will save the info about Hannah until mom and dad are off having their one-on-one chat about their day. I try hard not to mention it. Minutes after I finish setting the table, I ask Hazel to go up to get Hannah. Mick looks at me with concern in his eyes.

He grabs my hand. "How was your day?"

"Uh—fine—Dad."

He grabs my arm as I set the tortillas down.

"No really. I know I don't get to talk to you much—I'm trying really hard to make some changes with my job situation, but I need to know. Are you okay?"

I look into his deep blue eyes. For the first time in years, I can see that he sees me, so I answer honestly.

"Today was better than most. It was a pretty good day."

"Good. I'm glad." He gives me one of his crooked smiles, takes the bowl of lettuce and olives from my hands, and begins helping me set the table.

※※※

Dinner feels strange. I mean, everyone is pretty much themselves, but I feel different. I honestly want to hear about their day. Mick's lame jokes are even borderline funny tonight. Mom looks extra tired. Those dark blue crescent moons under her eyes, glaring at me from across the table, convinces me to volunteer to do the dishes, even though it's her turn.

Mick looks at me like he is seeing something magical. Truthfully, I'm even surprising myself.

Mom kisses me on my forehead as she starts off up the stairs.

"Thanks, Jo."

"It's the least I can do, since I've been home, *all day*."

Mom pauses on the stairs, Mick right on her heels. "Well, if you ever want to do something extremely productive during the day, all you have to do is ask."

"Extremely productive…" I roll my eyes as they disappear upstairs. What's that supposed to mean?

Hazel begins dumping the plates for me while I start loading the dishwasher. Hannah is slowly sweeping the floor, head hung low, silent. Hazel catches me staring at Hannah. She waves me down to get my attention and shakes her head, "no."

I guess now isn't a good time either. Hey, Hazel knows best.

When the entire kitchen is spotless, I take a long hot shower, feeling exhausted mentally—yet—free. I don't know why, but I just feel light and airy. I trudge into my room, taking in my nauseating walls.

I can repaint my room. That's productive! And it may keep my mind off school. I lay down on my bed. I'll mention it to Mom in the morning.

A gust of wind raises goosebumps on my arms as I pull up the covers. I look over at the window, but it's closed. I pull the comforter completely over my head. Shivering.

What in the world is going on, now? I slowly lower the comforter, curiosity getting the better of me. Then I see it. Small fragments of light in my peripheral vision. Afraid to look, I take a leap of faith.

"Adar? Is that you?"

Nothing.

I've seen him three times in the last few days why not keep the hallucination alive.

My core quivers. "Adar. Are you there?"

Yeah. I'm here.

Okay. I'm truly losing it. My breath is caught in my chest. Slowly I turn my head toward the voice.

There he is just as I have seen him—at school, across the street from Dr Brasser's office and in my dream—standing in the doorway of the bathroom the twins and I share.

I whip my head back around willing him to disappear. *It's all in my imagination. It's all in my imagination.*

I peek over my shoulder to find him now sitting against the wall.

Oh my God! I have lost it.

Adar sits forward. *Don't use His name in vain. It's disrespectful.*

Exhaling deeply, I jump out of bed and run right by this figment of my imagination.

What are you doing? he asks.

I don't answer him and head straight for the bathroom. I pull the bathroom door closed and lock it for extra security.

Oh—now you believe I'm real. He smiles with victory.

I sit back down on my bed, letting out the breath I had left in my chest. "Just in case you are real, I don't want one of my bratty sisters to see you. They would definitely run downstairs to tell my parents I have a guy in the room." I grin to lighten my mood.

He winks at me. *Good thinking. And good job!*

What?

You laughed. Laughter is good for you. It's like medicine.

He laughs loudly and I shush him drawing my index finger to my lips. He grins.

No worries, brushing me off like we are old friends, *No one can hear me, but you.*

He pulls something out of his pocket.

And they can't hear this either.

In his hand is the same small blue ball he had in the bathroom that day. He begins to bounce it and the soothing rhythm calms me. Why is he here again?

His eyes trained on the ball—he answers my question as if he knows my exact thoughts. *Grandma Ellis.*

Oh, how I enjoyed her when you guys used to hang out.

"Right. Because you are my—guardian angel. And she—summoned you?"

He shrugs his broad shoulders. *If that's what you want to call it.*

I roll my eyes. "So, what do you want, I'm pretty tired."

He smiles, then it fades as quickly as it appeared.

I must show you something.

"Wait." I press my palms to my head. "Don't you think I have had enough for one day? Can't this just wait until tomorrow, when I'm sure I will be in a better state of mind?"

I throw myself back in bed and throw the covers over my head.

Nope. This can't wait.

Pulling the cover down, I look over at him. His face is solemn.

Then a brilliant, fluorescent light spills into my room and I am consumed. Within seconds, I am standing in the middle of the hallway. It's still dark outside, but there's just a glimmer of royal-blue light coming from the window.

My dad comes flying out of the room, tie undone, and shirt half-buttoned, briefcase in hand. My mom runs to the banister, and yells down at him.

"Please don't rush, Mick. Take your time." When she turns around we are face to face, but she looks right through me.

"Honey, go wake up your sister. I will have to take you all to school today. Daddy had an emergency at work."

I turn to see Hazel standing right behind me. She wipes the sleep from her eyes.

"Yes, ma'am."

Adar's eyes are fixed on my mom as she walks back into her room. I follow her. She sits down on her bed and cups her face with both hands. Her shoulders slump. I can hear slow and steady sobs break through her hands.

There have only been two occasions that I can remember seeing my mom cry. The first was so long ago. The memory has become blurred with time. The second was the day she married Mick.

I remember sitting in the pew, being very careful not to dirty or wrinkle my pink chiffon dress. Mom and four other women, whom I can't remember, were all standing in a circle holding hands. They all wore pink gowns that hung off their shoulders and draped down to the floor. They looked like a gorgeous painting from a fancy museum—they took my breath away.

Mom looked like a vision from heaven. When she walked into the room everyone started to cry. To this day, I'm still not sure if it was because of how stunning she was. She was the only person in the room not crying.

She has never been an emotional person.

One of the women called me over to join them in the circle. My little pink dress with lace embellishments barely touched the floor. I felt like a real princess that day. We all held hands and the women began to pray. When the prayer was over, I looked up into my mom's hazel brown eyes and she was crying. When she noticed me looking—she touched my cheek.

"These are tears of joy, sweetie. I promise." She said.

My mind returns to the vision Adar is playing for me. I'm stunned. Seeing her cry knocks the life out of me a little bit. I hold my breath. I go to touch her hand, but my hand goes right through her. Adar gives me a warning look. He doesn't vocally say it, but it's like I can feel what he wants to say. I look back over at my mom. The tears have stopped, and she is now looking up at the ceiling. She says,

I know you don't hear from me much and I'm sorry for that. I have let the pain from my past drive me so much so that—I have no time to spare. I'm too busy for you. But, if you can just hear me now—please... If you could just listen— maybe—find a way to help us... I will make you a priority in

my life. I promise God…I will make room for you. We cannot make it without you. Please be with Mick. Protect him. Keep him safe for me and the girls. Send your angels to over shadow him. In Jesus' name. Amen.

She wipes her tears away and heads out into the hallway again—like nothing ever happened.

Hazel and Hannah are all dressed, but their hair is a mess. Mom exhales.

"I wish had a wand to just zap your hair into the perfect hair-do. Come on, let's get your hair together. We have to hurry."

"Aww, can't we just get a perm like you? It would make all of our lives easier."

"No." Mom retorts.

Hey where's Daddy. Why isn't he taking us to school?"

"Something really bad happened at work, honey. I can't tell you about it now, but it's pretty bad. I will have to take you today, so we have to hurry before I'm late."

"What about Jozi? Is she going to ride with us?"

"No, she sets an alarm. She should be fine. Let's let her get a little more sleep."

My thoughts start to run all over the place and I blink for what seems like the longest minute in history. When I open my eyes, I am in a large building with at least twenty people speed-walking in several different directions. The walls are white, the floors are white and the majority of the people zooming through the hallways are wearing white.

I spin around in a circle looking for a familiar face. Then I see him. Mick. He flies through one of the doors, heading straight for the receptionist, sweating and out of breath.

"I'm here to see, Jasmine Porter…"

Another lady at the desk, sitting juxtapose to the receptionists, turns around and stands. She looks calm, but the expression on her face says something entirely different.

"Right this way."

She silently escorts Mick to a waiting room. I follow. In the waiting room are a hand full of people. Two women in a corner by the window are holding on to each other, weeping uncontrollably. Several others are spread out around the room crying hysterically. Mick walks in slowly and a women with salt and pepper hair bearing an expression of pure despair walks up to him. She stares him right in the eyes as if she could kill him with just one gaze. Then, she whips back her right hand and slaps my dad with a thunderclap of her palm.

Hard.

So hard it takes my breath away. Hard enough the sound draws the attention of everyone in the waiting room. Every look drawn from that slap, signals an even bigger attack. They all seem to recognize him, and begin to shoot looks that could kill of their own.

Mick stalls. He is motionless. One hand cupping his jaw and the other held up in defense, He is unaware of the others who are now surrounding him.

"You did this." She yells into Mick's face. "You killed my baby!"

She draws her hand back once more and begins an onslaught of one hit after another. I jolt into action, trying to shield him from the hits, but it is no use. An aged man, who seems to be well beyond Mick's age, grabs the older women's flailing arms. Once she realizes who has stopped her, she breaks down into his arms.

"This will not bring her back, Helen." He repeats this as he walks her over to a nearby chair, "This will not bring our baby back."

Mick feebly lifts his head. His face is a pained red and his eyes bear the stress of the world. Slowly he takes in the room and the dark stares of the bystanders who just watched the violent attack.

He holds out a hand toward them all, "I'm sorry." He cries out. "My God—I am so sorry."

No one moves. Mick backs away toward the door. Defeated.

When he pushes the door open, I am thrown into a tunnel of light and transported back to my bedroom. I sit up on my bed in haste, my eyes darting around the room. It takes me a moment to recognize where I am. My heart is pounding. My breath is coming out in heaves.

Calm down, Jozi. Calm down.

"How," I pant for air. "How do you expect me to be calm when you just showed me that? What was that about?"

Adar kneels down right in front of me. For the first time I see him close up—smooth almond-colored skin, without a blemish in sight, emerald green eyes that move like the ocean. The outline of his body almost appears to be vibrating. My heartbeat slows to a steady bass drum.

I am sorry. He hangs his head. *This is always tough for me too. I shouldn't have allowed you to see so much so quickly. But time is of the essence. Are you okay?*

He places one hand on my back, shaking his head. Clearly beating himself up.

"I think I'm okay, Adar."

He sits down right in front of me. He doesn't say a word.

"So, what was that all about?"

I thought maybe you could put—how do you humans say it—two and two together.

I don't think, I just blurt it out. "Did someone die? Jasmine? Did she die?"

Yes.

"Who was she? What does she have to do with Mick?"

She was a witness in Mick's current case. The case he won recently and celebrated a few weeks ago.

I think about that for a moment. Then it all hits me like a bucket of ice cold water. My eyes grow wide. Adar glares at me.

The police have not found the murderer. Your father carries the weight of Jasmine's death on his shoulders. Her entire family blames him for all of it and he doesn't blame them for feeling that way.

Tears begin to sting the back of my eyes. The gaping hole I felt just a few days ago opens wider. It hadn't gone away. All this time I could sense it lurking in the corners of my mind, waiting for the right time to suck me in again.

Now, now, Jozi. Don't let it lure you in. Stay in control.

He begins to bounce that stupid blue ball.

I flinch at the soothing sound of it hitting the wall, clenching my fists,

"I am in control! Now, can you please stop bouncing that ball!"

He doesn't.

I begin to think about that particular day. All I could think about was myself—how I was late for school and my non-existent relationship with Ky. All the while, Mick was going through so much more. And, I was blaming him for something he had no control over. And Mom! No wonder she was so awful towards me that evening.

But, you see, even now you are injecting your story into his. He had no idea how you felt that day. Everything that happened was drowned out by this tragedy. You had your version of the most horrible day and he had his.

I grab my head in anguish. "What do you mean, Adar? You are speaking in riddles."

Swiping the ball from mid-air, Adar kneels to face me.

What I mean is, take yourself out of the story. Think about what he needs at this very moment, not what you did wrong. Focus on him.

He sits back down and begins throwing the ball up to the ceiling.

That day is over. You can only live for today.

Mick. He hid his pain so effortlessly today and every day since. He must still feel awful about what happened. I could never have done that. Looking over at Adar, I am transfixed by the small blue sphere flying back and forth between his hand and the ceiling. How is he doing it?

My thoughts slow down for a moment. The tranquil peace that Adar always seems to bring with him has returned. I fall back onto my bed to soak it all up.

"Why did Mick come home early today?"

He got off early. His boss made him take a leave of absence until everything dies down. He didn't argue. He thought it would be a good opportunity to spend more time with you.

"How do you even do that?"

Do what?

"Know when to appear—know everything about everybody?"

Adar shrugs his broad, muscular shoulders, which makes him look more like just one of the guys. Normal.

I don't know, he says. *I'm just doing my job.*

He smiles, then gets up from his sitting position.

I have to go now, but I won't go too far.

I sit up as quick as I can, and within one flutter of my eye lids, he's gone—like a vapor. The only things left are me, the peace Adar left, and the tinge of guilt pulsating within my heart.

No, I protest. This is not about me.

18 | Two Are Better Than One

My eyes fly open at the sound of a faint whisper. Hovering right over me is a small presence bearing down on my shoulders. I blink twice to get my eyes to focus.

"Jozi, wake up."

I flail my arms, willing the whisperer to go away. Just when I'm about to fall back to sleep, the hands begin to shake my shoulders. I come to my senses fully and shoot up into a sitting position, annoyed that I am awake.

The person in front of me comes into focus. Hazel.

She is all dressed, but her hair is still a garbled mess. I glance out the window at the dim gray sky. It's still too early for Mom to be awake. Hazel's tight spiral curls shoot out in several directions, some draping her face making her look three-years-old again.

In the middle of an achy stretch, I groan, "What is it, Hazel?"

She looks at the door like someone is going to walk through at any moment, then looks back at me.

"I finally found out what's been going on with Hannah."

I straighten.

"Okay, so what is it?"

She comes in closer to me, so close, I can smell the lilac Johnson & Johnson bath wash Mom makes them use to fall asleep. It's strange, but I get this weird urge to pull her in for a hug like I used to do when they were babies. I ward off that crazy thought.

"So, there's this girl—she lives about five houses down. Her name is—Tera—I think. She just moved here and she's in Hannah's homeroom class and her music class. She also rides the same bus as us. According to Hannah, since she moved here, Tera's been picking on her."

Hazel stops and takes a quick glance at the door.

"She told me that in the lunch line Tera always ends up behind her. She whispers in Hannah's ear, 'Wannabe.'"

"What is that supposed to mean?" I frown.

"It means that Hannah is a NO-body!" Hazel sucks her teeth and rolls her eyes like I should know this already. "It means that she doesn't know who she is, so she's pretending to be someone else!"

I shrug and then fold my arms. Why would such a small thing make Hannah so upset?

"Well, that's the case for every twelve-year-old, teen, and young adult, Hazel! What's the big deal?"

She stamps her foot and turns her back towards me, "See, this is why we never tell you nothing."

It's not about me, I say to myself. *It's not about how I see things.*

"Hazel, all I'm saying is, it's okay not to know who you are yet. That takes time. And this Terror girl…"

She interrupts, "It's Tera, T-E-R—"

"I know how it's spelled, Hazel!" I take a deep breath and correct myself for the sake of my point. "This *Tera* doesn't even know who *she* is yet."

Hazel exhales deeply, "I know, but Hannah said she says it around all of her friends, and they all start to laugh. I think she calls her that because our dad is white."

"She's just jealous, Hazel. That's all. You two are going to have to deal with people like her all your life. You think I didn't have to deal with that? Hey! I still do! Look at me, I have no complexion and my hair looks like a lion's mane!"

Hazel starts to laugh. I begin to laugh with her. Throwing my arm about her shoulders, I realize her laugh has now turned into sobs. I feel the sting of what I just said. My mom used to do the same thing to me when I was growing up—having to deal with being in between—neither completely black nor white.

She would say, "Ignore them. You know who you are."

The only problem with that is—it doesn't stop them from being mean.

I used to think maybe my mom's life was so messed up when she was growing up, she had no choice but to grow tough skin. Skin she felt we needed to grow in order to survive a public-school education. What she doesn't know is this is where all of my suicidal thoughts started. This was the beginning of that enormous black hole in the back of my mind. My temperature begins to rise at the thought of Hannah beginning the same downward spiral.

"Stop crying, Hazel, please," I squeeze her a little tighter, trying to come up with a plan of action.

"But that's not it, Jo. That's not why she came home crying yesterday.

"Well, what happened?"

"Yesterday, when I thought she was running late to get on the bus, she had already gotten on."

"Okay. That's a good thing, right?"

"Well, Tera got on before me and sat right next to Hannah. Hannah said she took a hand full of her hair and pulled it tight around her hand. She said…"

Hazel sucks in a big breath of air, and she can hardly get the words out.

"She said Tera didn't let go until it was time for all of us to get off the bus."

I stand to my feet. My hands ball up into tight fists. It takes all Dr. Brasser's breathing exercises to not lay my fist into the nearest wall. I pace the length of my room.

"Why didn't she tell the bus driver, Hazel? Why didn't she yell out—or do something?"

"Because she knows snitching only makes things worse. Worse things have happened to our friend Robby. He told on his bully and now he's being homeschooled because it got so bad."

Now, as still as a statue, I get an idea of what I need to do. I walk over to Hazel. I look her right in her pretty hazel-green eyes.

"Look, two are better than one. We have to let this Tera know that Hannah has two sisters who are more than willing to do what needs to be done to protect Hannah."

Hazel bats her eyes. "What do you mean, Jozi?"

"Fight, silly!"

"Oh!" She finally gets where I'm going with this and stands to her feet, "Yeah! That's right!"

I laugh at her innocence. "Alright, now go wake Hannah up and Mom too. I think you two should ride the bus to school today."

"No, Jozi. We hate riding the bus if we don't have to. Dad's going to take us."

"No, Dad is off today. He's going to rest. I will walk you to the bus stop and I will ride the bus with you, if I have to."

I drop my voice to a whisper. "Remember. Whatever it takes to protect our sister."

She peers up at me.

"Right."

Hazel walks towards the door with her head hanging low, then stops. She turns around, tears rolling down her face again. "What are you going to do?"

"You will see. Just put your game-face on."

"What's a 'game-face?'"

"A face that says The Skies Sisters are not to be messed with."

19 | The Bully

I hurry to get dressed. I throw on my gray hoodie—since I can't find my red one—and a pair of skinny jeans, then head over to Hannah's room. She argues with me the entire time mom is doing Hazel's hair, but by that time Hazel has already told mom and dad, who both agree that it's time for them to start riding the bus to school.

Now busy slicking Hannah's hair up into a tight bun, mom gives me a side glance. "What's gotten into you, Jo?"

I lean up against the bathroom door, waving away the citrus-scented hairspray. "What do you mean, Mom?"

She looks more rested. Her new pixie cut makes her look five years younger. When she cut all seventeen inches of her hair a few weeks ago, we all thought she was going through some kind of mid-life crisis.

"Why are you being so—nice?"

"What are you talking about?" I shrug. "Just because I can't stand to be around these annoying little pests, doesn't mean it will get rid of them. I'm stuck. What's the point in fighting it?"

I push Hannah as she leaves the bathroom. She smells like a fresh glass of lemonade. Hazel nudges me from behind, then heads down the stairs behind Hannah. I let a little laugh escape my mouth, actually hoping she didn't take me seriously. Somewhere deep inside, I guess I do care about their feelings.

Mom leaves for work just before we head down to the bus stop. As we walk out the door, I coach Hannah and Hazel on "The Look."

"See, when you are dealing with a bully you can't let them sense fear. If they do, you are in for a long school year. Believe me—been there, done that."

They both look at each other with wide eyes.

"Yeah, believe it or not, I haven't always been so tough. Now, like I said, show no fear. Look them in their eyes. Let them know you are not *the* one. Demand respect. Most bullies want to hurt others because they are hurting."

Dr. Brasser told me this once she found out I was bullied in junior high and well into my freshman year of high school.

"They also will leave you alone if they don't have anyone backing them. Or, if you have friends who have your back. And by the way, if your so-called friends aren't taking up for you, you need new ones!"

I stop walking and turn to face Hannah. I point my finger directly at Hazel's chest, "You see this girl right here? This is your best friend." I point my finger at Hannah's chest, and I look in Hazel's eyes, "You see this girl right here? This is *your* best friend. So, it doesn't matter if your other friends don't have your back. You have each other." I start back walking. "You're lucky. I didn't have anyone."

When we get closer to the bus stop, Hazel points out Tera. She's almost my height which is a foot taller than the twins. She has my mom's complexion and has the body of a teenager.

"Wow! Why does this girl look like she should be in high school?"

I guess they know it's rhetorical, because they don't bother answering me.

Her hair is pulled back into a tight ponytail which makes her eyes look squinty and malicious. When the three of us walk up, everything goes quiet. A boy Tera is playing around with gestures in our direction. She immediately takes us all in, then rolls her eyes.

I whisper behind my back. "No fear."

They follow as I walk directly up to her. I'm close enough to see that her pupils are dilated.

I don't waste any time. "Do you have a problem with my sister?"

She recoils, trying to step back to get a better look at me, but I step forward. The kids waiting at the bus stop feel the tension in the air and begin to make the typical "fight circle."

Tera furrows her brow. "I don't know what you are talking about."

"Yes, you do," I say calmly.

I look her up and down, noticing her dirty jeans, and the hole in the front of her shoe. Refocusing my attention on her eyes, I see something. Fear.

She rolls her head and steps closer to me. "No—I—don't."

I don't back down. I stand firm and from the looks of it, the twins aren't backing down either. They haven't moved from their position.

"Now look, I didn't yell at you. So, don't yell at me."

She sucks her teeth and rolls her neck, looking over at the boy who looks much younger than the twins.

"Now you see these two girls standing behind me?"

She doesn't look.

I continue anyway, speaking very slowly so she hears every word.

"There will be no more name calling to either of them. You will never touch another hair on their beautiful little heads, let alone breath in their direction. Matter of fact, I don't want you within ten feet of them."

She folds her arms and shifts her weight. "Please. I'm not scared of you. She rolls her eyes."

I tear my gaze away and respond over my shoulder, "You should be."

As I break through the ridiculous circle, I feel the twins' presence behind me. We walk a few feet away from the crowd and I can see her watching us. When her eyes meet mine, she turns her back to us and continues her conversation with the boy.

Hazel looks at me. Her arms are folded and the disappointment behind her rigid expression is very obvious.

"So, how is *that*," she gestures in Tera's direction, "going to help Hannah?"

I told you, I have been through this. I know what I'm doing.

Hannah chimes in, hanging her head. "Your threatening her is only going to get you in trouble, Jo, and make it worse for me."

My stomach fills with the nausea of guilt. I tilt Hannah's head up.

"No, it's not, and don't do that. Remember, The Look," I whisper. "I didn't threaten her. I just told her what she was not going to do. She is probably imagining the consequences, but I didn't tell her I was going to smash her face in"

"That's true," Hazel shrugs.

"Anyway, I have one more thing to do before I go."

Hannah fidgets with her bookbag straps. "And what is that?"

"I need to talk to your bus driver."

Within seconds, the bus arrives. All of the kids file on, Tera is one of the first to board.

"See? She's trying to stay far away from you already." I wink.

Hazel and Hannah are the last two to board, then I get on. When the bus driver notices me, she frowns in confusion.

"I know, I know. I am not a passenger. I am here to let you know there was a student assaulted on your bus yesterday. That student was my sister. She is being harassed by that—" I point to Tera, sitting all the way in the back of the bus, "girl in the purple shirt."

I cross my arms and stare the bus driver down. "My dad, Defense Attorney, Skies, would appreciate it if you payed closer attention to your passengers and make sure that girl, in the purple shirt, doesn't sit wherever she wants."

The bus driver, looking in the rear-view mirror at Tera, purses her lips, and nods.

"Okay, I got it. Thanks for letting me know."

I glance down at Hannah and Hazel, who are sitting in the seat right behind the bus driver. They both wink at me as I get off. The doors flap shut behind me and the bus driver begins to speak over the intercom—*There will be assigned seating when you board this afternoon. And, Tera Wilson, report to the office as soon as we arrive at school.*

Feeling accomplished, I smile for the one good deed done for the day. I turn and walk back to the house, happy Hannah will have a much better day.

The breeze blowing through the trees tickles my cheeks and my smile grows even bigger. I don't know exactly who I'm talking to, but I find myself speaking out loud.

"Please let them have a good day."

It just comes out like I have been doing it my whole life. In that moment, a whisper of the wind says to me, *I have it from here.* My steady pace slows a bit, just as I reach the front door. A sigh of relief breaks through my lips.

"Thanks." I whisper back and go into the house.

20 | Ten More Days

When the twins got home yesterday, they wouldn't leave my side. It turns out, my little Oscar winning performance worked. Tera stayed away from them and even started spreading a rumor about their "big bully" sister.

I don't care. She can call me whatever she wants, as long as she leaves my sisters alone.

When Mick finally woke up for the day, I told him about my productive idea to repaint my room. He was ecstatic and thought we should do it together since we both were going to be home. I wanted to say no, but I remembered what Adar said about Mick wanting to spend time with me.

Reluctantly, I came with him to the home improvement store to pick out a color. The first color he suggests is this hideous and a cross between lilac and grayish purple. I gag at the sight of it. This is the reason I did not want his help.

He laughs. "What? What's wrong with it?"

"No more little girl colors, Dad. I am tired of the stereotypical girly colors. For the past three years, my Pepto-Bismol walls have made me hate even sleeping in my room. At this point, I am completely against any color in the pink and purple family."

I want a color that would make me feel light and airy. A color that would take me to a faraway place, when I need to get there fast. I want to be able to walk into my room and feel like I'm taking off to that place—leaving all of my cares behind.

After hours of indecisiveness I decided on a shade of blue. The cute sales clerk said it was called bice. To me, that sounded like a pro-wrestler's stage name, but it was beautiful.

It reminded me of the Hawaiian sky I adored when we visited, two summers ago. Mick had some vacation time and surprised us all with a week getaway. It took a lot of negotiating and whining to get mom to go, but she finally caved. Mick, on the other hand, spent all but one day in the hotel room, working on a case.

Mick insisted I also get a pint of yellow paint for the sun. At first, I argued with him about. I thought it was a childish idea, but I gave in when he brought up the idea of it being a team effort. He made himself responsible for the sun. Slowly, this became a brilliant idea when I remembered how he painted intricate little flowers all around the border of the twin's room. I was shocked at how good it turned out. So, he may be capable of creating something I like.

By the end of the day, we all ended up in my room, preparing it for the huge paint project tomorrow. The twins helped, by sweeping and taking down the curtains before they left to prepare our dinner for the night. Pizza.

Dad was so tired from taping the room off and moving all the heavy furniture that he left, before I could even thank him. Mom and I find ourselves sitting on the dusty hardwood floor, decluttering my desk of all the short stories I have jotted down over the past three years.

"Jozi, why don't you write these down in a notebook or something, or maybe even in a Word document? I mean, that's what normal writers do."

I gently take them away from her and stack the sheets neatly.

"No, I like the way the ink looks on the stationary Grandma Ellis bought me. It makes the experience of writing feel more—*authentic*."

I walk into the hallway and place them in one of my empty dresser drawers.

Mick moved every piece of furniture out of my room except for my bed and my tiny desk. We settled on moving my full-size bed into the middle of the room so we could easily get around it.

Mom hands me the last stack of stories, then slowly peels herself up off the floor, groaning in the process.

Limping over to the bed, she says to me.

"Why did you let me do that? Why did I do that?"

"What?" I laugh.

"Why did you let me sit down on that floor?" She purses her lips and exhales with pleasure as she sits down on the bed.

She pats the space next to her as I shut the drawer. Groaning, I sit down anyway. I knew this was coming, I just didn't know when.

"Jozi, have you called your grandmother lately?"

I pick at my bitten-down nails. "No."

"I see."

I look over at her nails. They're not manicured or painted because she's a nurse, but they look so much neater than mine. I admire them. Her long thin fingers clasped together, slowly pressing into each other. She's worried.

What's wrong with her? Is she okay?"

"Well, she's getting old and…"

"And what?" My heart sinks into my stomach.

"You just don't want to take anyone for granted. I have been thinking about going to visit her myself, just to take a little break from work and spend some time with her, but…"

"But what, Mom? You should go." I look up at her, sure of myself.

"No," she says, shaking her head, "I think you need to go."

My eyes grow big. For a moment, I get a little excited, but then the hot ball of anger nestled inside of me bounces up.

"No, thank you. You go. She's your mom and you definitely need to take a break."

I turn my head away from her, unwilling to hear any more about this. I look out the window. Although the sun just came out an hour ago, the clouds are already beginning to close their curtain on it, which gives the sky this dark rusty orange color. Oh, how I love Seattle.

Despite my resolute tone, she doesn't give up.

"No, I think you should go. I will get out there this summer. You just happen to be *conveniently* out of school…,"

She gives me her sarcastic smirk that I hate so much, then stands.

"This would be a great time for you two to—talk."

Just as I'm about to protest this idea with every ounce of energy I have left in me, an image of Grandma Ellis on her knees, crying out for me, projects right before my eyes. My shoulders lower, my chest caves in, and I am humbled at the thought of her caring so much about such an unlovable girl.

"Okay, Mom. I will go." I look up at her, and smile. "When do you think we should book the tickets?"

Her perfectly arched eyebrows almost touch her hairline. She's surprised, but also smiling from ear to ear.

"Oh, you're leaving the day after tomorrow."

"What!"

She laughs out loud, "Yep. Your dad and I talked about it yesterday and we both thought this would be good for you. I knew you would give in. You miss her and you know you do."

I'm a little salty she would make this all seem like a choice, only to sucker me into it. I fold my arms and stare at the floor.

She sits back down next to me. "Come on Jozi. You need to get away from everything, too. It will be good for the both of you."

As she rubs circles on the small of my back. I give in.

"Okay. But, I'm not apologizing to her."

She quickly stands again. "No apologies necessary. She can't wait to see you."

I start. "She knows already?"

Mom leaves the room almost dancing and I can't help but to feel duked. I do miss Grandma Ellis. That cold, empty space in my heart where her love used to reside pulses.

The harsh pain brings tears to my eyes and I long for today to end. My pride pushed aside, to be one step—one day closer to filling that space again feels amazing.

21 | Nine More Days

Nine more days until I return to school. My feeble attempts to stop counting the days have been useless. Every morning when I wake up, the first thing that comes to mind is how much closer I am to the dreaded day. I feel darkness closing in around me. And, involuntarily I'm reminded of Adar.

Adar, the reason I'm still here. Adar, a figment of my imagination, but—he seems more real than anything else right now.

It's scary to think about him, because although I'm sure he is real, there's a part of me that still believes he's not. At any rate, the thought him being real is comforting.

Maybe after I spend some time, in Maryland, with Grandma Ellis, it will all become clearer. Maybe the confusion will leave me, and I can once again feel normal.

Having to sit with Dr. Brasser for an hour is horrific enough. Getting institutionalized for hallucinations would be unbearable.

Today, I have to pay Dr. Brasser another visit, per my stipulations to return to school. Mom dropped me off just ten minutes ago. I guess grocery shopping takes precedence over my sanity, but whatever.

Dr. Brasser's current patient must have more issues than I do. Their session is going long. My session should have started by now. Tapping my foot on the gray tile and fidgeting with the draw strings on my hoodie, doesn't give me the calm that I need. I should have brought some stationary.

I shiver as the air vent kicks on. One of the main reasons I hate coming to see Dr. Brasser is her office always feels like the Arctic. It doesn't matter that I have on an under shirt, a shirt, and a hoodie. I always shiver the entire time I'm here.

As I study the awful painting on the wall in front of me, a warm breeze sweeps across my face. I glance up at the glossy canvas. It is splotched with blues and greens, creating something that looks like a calm ocean. It reminds me of Adar's eyes. I glance away and there, in the corner of the small waiting room, is a mirage of light. I blink several times to focus my eyes, but it does no good. The haze of radiant light only becomes more defined. I know within an instant.

It's him.

Then, I realize I'm not shivering anymore. I feel—warm.

I take a quick glance over at Dr. Brasser's receptionist, who is so busy clacking away on the keyboard she hasn't noticed *it*. At least, she hasn't noticed me staring at *it* either. A part of me wants to get up and walk over to talk to examine *it*, but I hesitate. I get a strange feeling that maybe it isn't Adar. The last time we were together he could hear my thoughts, and I could sense his.

Yeah, you spotted me. You are getting good at this.

My heart jumps in my chest at the sound of his voice. The receptionist peeks up at me from her small round glasses. With an irritated look on her face, she doesn't falter, she continues to type.

Adar. I shoot the receptionist a furtive look. *What are you doing here?*

Just checking on you. You are one of my priorities these days. What's up?

The receptionist is still oblivious to my telepathic conversation. So weird.

Uh, I'm waiting to be seen by my doctor.

Adar steps out of the light and his body comes fully in view. He eyes me and folds his arms. He taps his foot as if to say, "I'm waiting."

I give in. I know what he's asking. *I'm pretty good, I think. I'm better than I've been in a while."*

Good.

Dr. Brasser's door opens abruptly. A tall girl storms out into the waiting area and shuts the door behind her. I shift in my seat. She notices me and gives me a sharp stare. She's tall and slender, with paper thin blond hair that reaches her elbow.

"Good luck," she mumbles as she leaves the office in a quick stride.

I look over at Adar, who has a giddy smirk on his face. He shrugs his shoulders, then walks back into the light and just like that—he's gone. I smirk. He just shows up and then leaves just as soon as he came, like it's normal.

"Jozi?" Dr. Brasser calls out to me. She is standing in the door way of her office.

Startled, I respond with a very small, "Yes?"

"I am ready to see you now."

I get up in a hurry, because the sooner I get in there the sooner I can be done with her. Usually I see her twice a month. Twice a week is just too much. By the time she closes the door, I am already reclined in the coffee-colored leather chair.

She walks over to the nearby cushioned chair, her legal pad and pen in hand. Good. We are getting straight to business.

"So, let's recap our last session, shall we?"

"Sure," I agree quickly.

"Last time we met we discussed your incident at school. You shared how angry Rowan made you feel. You confessed that you lost time, meaning you blacked out and you don't remember the assault."

Wow. She just accused me of assault. Great. Very encouraging. I take my eyes off the ceiling and look at her. She is reading from her notes, glasses tucked down on the tip of her nose. I exhale deeply, willing myself to keep quiet. No arguing for me today.

"You did not feel any remorse and said, I quote, 'She deserved it.'"

She pauses for a moment to flip the page. "Then, you shared your encounter with a man who appeared in the girl's bathroom, whom you think is your guardian angel. Am I correct?"

I smile wide. It was so satisfying to get her all tangled up in a tizzy. She probably even considered if she has just happened to make me crazier.

"Yep!"

"So, after our discussion about hallucinations and how anxiety—along with depression—can cause unexpected sightings, are you still convinced that he was real?"

Oh my gosh! If I keep this up, she just may want to see me more often. Better to keep Adar to myself.

"No. I don't think he's real. I do think that I was hallucinating that day."

"And why is that?"

Wow, she's never satisfied.

"Well, because I haven't seen him anymore."

"Hmm."

I look over at her, straining to see what she's writing.

"And, I think that was just a very depressing day for me. I felt like I was in a dark tunnel, wandering around all day, desperate to find the light at the end."

She looks at me, dead on, and I can tell she believes me because it's the first time she's looked at me all day.

We finish the session talking about my biological father. She asks if I've thought about him lately. I tell her no, even though his absence claws at my consciousness daily. She asks if I have confided in my mom or asked her about him.

I tell her that I never plan on asking, but she says that the only way I can find closure is by knowing the truth—the entire story behind why he left.

I tell her I will try—mainly because I don't want to spend one more second in her cold, depressing office.

22 | Tomorrow

I'm so excited tomorrow is the day I get to see Grandma Ellis, I jump out of bed to brush my teeth and get right to prepping my base boards for all the painting Mick and I have to do today. My clock and cell phone are out in the hallway with my dresser, so I have no idea what time it is. By the look of the light casting into my room, it's probably close to noon.

A knock comes through the door, just as I retrieve the tape from under my bed.

"Come in!"

Mick cracks the door and peeks his head in, "Can I come in?"

"Sure," I stand up straight and wave him in.

"So, do you trust me?"

I furrow my brow and walk over to him, "Uh, sometimes. Why do you ask that?"

His face looks pure and honest as he opens the door completely, revealing just the shoulder of someone in the hallway.

I duck my head around the corner, trying to see who it is, but he jumps in front of me. "Well, as you know, I would like to think that one of my gifts is creating—well painting?"

"Yes..." I try to out-wit him by moving to the other side to catch a glimpse of the person in the hallway. I fail.

"Right, so I was wondering if you would trust me to paint your room while you go out for a bit. Then, when you get back, you can pack and prepare for your trip."

I cut my eyes at him, wondering what he's up to.

"Why are you guys being so…"

Mick smirks at me, gives me a sly wink.

"…nice? What's the catch?"

"Jo." He steps into the room, closing the door behind him, leaving whoever is in the hallway all alone. "I realize I haven't been—present…" Mick's eyes search my face. "Can you let me do this one thing for you? I feel like I owe you much more, but I promise you won't regret leaving this with me."

In his eyes, I can see so much regret and sadness. I just want to break down and cry in his arms. He's going through so much, yet he wants to do something for me.

Wow.

I don't cry. I don't even hug him like I really want to. I hold back because who knows how long this kindness and attention will last.

Instead, I extend my hand and say, "Okay, Dad. Have at it."

Mick smiles. And gives me another one of his signature winks. He kisses me on my cheek, then opens the door. Just like that, Kyell slips in just as my dad closes the door behind him.

"Hi, Jo."

My heart jolts in my chest. It's beating so loud I can hear it behind my ears.

"What are you doing here?"

I wince at the sound of my voice. The question comes out a little too nice. I haven't heard from my supposed best friend in a few days, and I'm the one who was betrayed.

"I just wanted to see you before you head off across the country."

"Wow. My parents tell you everything. Did they tell you I've loved you my whole life, too?"

I drop my head, pushing my tangled curls behind my ear. OMG! I hope he didn't hear that. I don't dare to look up at him.

"Wanna take a walk with me?" he asks, as if I never said a word.

"Uh, I guess." I look down at my Minnie Mouse pjs. "Just let me get dressed first."

"Great!" Slowly, he walks over to the door. "Okay, I will be downstairs having some of your mom's famous blueberry waffles."

Kyell's footsteps thunder down the stairs. I hesitate. Re-thinking my decision to go with him. Why do I give him this much power over me? Has he even considered the last thing I said to him? I feel like a fool. He is completely ignoring how I feel and I am allowing it.

Before I can even take two steps toward the bathroom, I realize Mick is standing at the door again. He looks at me with concern in his eyes.

I stop in my tracks, "What now, Dad?"

"I know you like him."

I roll my eyes. He doesn't know the half of it, at least I don't think he does. On the other hand, he is a lawyer which means he has a knack for reading people.

Tears well up in my eyes.

I look up. "I love him, Dad."

He walks over to me and puts one hand on my face.

"Jo, I love that you have someone that you can talk to and count on. That's why I've always been okay with him coming around. I trust him as your friend. He's always been a great—*friend*."

I sniff and wipe away a few stray tears. "Just spit it out, Dad. I can take it."

"I knew the day would come when I saw you look at someone the way you look at Ky. I just didn't know it would be so soon." He looks down as if to search for more words. "I just didn't know it would be him.

"He's my best friend. My only friend."

"And that's exactly my point. There's so many more boys out there that I'm sure would value your affection, Jo."

I exhale in frustration. "Dad, just say it."

"I haven't seen that look in his eyes, Jo." He quickly looks at me. "Now, don't get me wrong, Kyell is a good kid. He really cares about you. It just seems he loves being your friend."

He looks at me with concern. "Just be careful."

"O-kay. I will."

Too late. This walk is going to be all about what I told him.

He kisses me on my forehead. Then, slowly leaves, closing the door behind him.

⁕⁕⁕

It takes me longer than I expected to get dressed because for the first time in five days, I actually care about finding something nice to wear. Despite the brief talk with my dad still replaying in my head, I'm excited to see Ky.

I push past my disappointment in him and focus on the good. He's here! Oh, how I have missed his corny jokes and coy smile. I'm so excited I can't get down the stairs fast enough. I tumble down the last two almost plunging into the wall.

"Wow, Jo. What's up with you?" Hazel chirps. Always the one to have something to say.

"Hush up, Hazel. Don't start." I give her the look and point a stern finger at her.

"Okay—okay," she whines, throwing her hands up and then continuing to eat her cheerios.

I look over at Ky, who is sitting right next to her. He is laser focused on finishing his waffles. Hannah is giggling at the whole commotion and peeking up at me as if she knows something I don't. Mom is in another world, washing the waffle iron, humming some tune.

"Good morning, Mom."

"Good morning, Jo." She points to a small, red container on the counter. "I put the extra waffles in the microwave and the eggs are in there."

"Okay. I can eat when we come back. Come on, Ky." I motion for him to get up.

Mom looks at me with questioning eyes. Dad is finally coming down the stairs and sees the look mom is giving me. He makes eye contact with me, and whispers something in her ear.

Weird. Mom nods her head, agreeing with whatever he said. Walking over to the twins, she grips them around their shoulders.

"Okay, girls, make sure you wash your dishes and clean up your rooms. I will be home around six."

They both moan and plead with her to stay.

"No, I promised Sarah I would cover her shift." She gives them a weak smile. "But, I'm off tomorrow."

"Okaaaay," they moan.

She kisses their foreheads, then walks over to me. "See you tonight? I'll help you pack?"

"Okay."

Then she kisses my forehead before she heads upstairs to get dressed. Dad sits down at the table with a plate already prepared and filled with eggs, bacon and waffles. Ky looks over at him as we walk towards the door.

"I will have her back in an hour, Mr. Skies."

Dad answers around a mouthful of waffles. "Take your time. I'm here all day."

✥⚜✥

We walk through the neighborhood catching up on what has been going on in class. Kyell tries to assure me that I'm not missing much.

"I brought you all of the work from your classes. It's not much. You can get it done in a day."

"Awesome. I will finish it in Maryland. Just email me the assignments for next week."

"No problem," he says. "So, are you excited to get away for a little while?"

"Yes. Very!"

We walk up to a bench in the neighborhood park. It's overcast, but the sun is peeking shyly through the clouds.

"I think it's a great idea, Jo. You know? To get away. I wish I could go with you." He says as he takes a seat on the bench.

He looks over at me and I look at him, searching his eyes to see if he actually means it. Then, he laughs. My heart sinks into my stomach. He didn't mean it for one second.

I lean forward, digging my feet into the gravel, contemplating what has been going on with him the last few days. I hesitate to ask because I really don't want to know, but he begins to speak without any prompting.

"So, Zeem told me you guys texted a few times."

"Yeah." I don't look at him. "We have chatted a couple of times. I figured you put him up to it."

"No. Actually, I haven't. He offered up the information when I mentioned how worried I was about you." He nudges me. "Because you weren't responding to my texts."

"Do you blame me? You told Shelly my deepest, darkest secret. A secret I didn't even tell you. Now, I'm suspended and probably the topic of discussion on Facebook, Twitter Snapchat and INSTAGRAM!"

He looks me in my eyes. "No. I don't blame you. Zeem is a good person to talk to, so I was happy he was capable of reaching you."

I begin running through the conversation Zeem and I had. I imagine his slanted dark eyes staring back at me. My heart flutters. The feeling is warm and comforting.

"It's fine, though." He kicks at a large rock near his foot. "I've been thinking about what you said."

I sit up. My eyes dart away from him, trying not to make eye contact. The calm I had disappears.

"What about it?"

He stands up, then walks over to a nearby oak to pull a leaf off. He examines it. "Well, you know…about how you feel."

I study my used to be white Vans.

He starts, "How long have you felt this way."

"I don't know, Ky. It's cliché to say it this way, but it kind of snuck up on me."

He walks back over toward me. My eyes meet his. For a moment, I am thrown into a fantasy world that I have traveled to many times over the past few years.

He diverts the conversation, as if what I have just confessed didn't matter.

"I don't understand why you are so upset, Jo. If we could all just sit down together and talk this through, I'm sure we could find a common ground."

Thrown off and completely confused, I stand up and move in just a little closer, to be sure I am hearing him correctly.

"What are you talking about, Ky."

Little kids in the distance stop and stare because my volume and tone have just taken a violent turn. Their parents coax them to keep playing.

He stretches his hands out—motioning for me to bring it down. "The only reason I told Shelly is because she's your friend, too. I thought we both could keep an eye on you. You know, to help you through this."

I squint my eyes at him. He's so blind. More blind than I thought.

"Really? We are back at square one? You can't even see how toxic she is? That you are so infatuated with her you don't realize what she has done."

Ky begins to talk with his hands. Now I know he's upset, but I couldn't care less.

"What? What has she done, Jozi? It seems that everyone is always doing something to you. You are always the victim."

I recoil at those words. I count backwards from ten to zero. When I reach zero, I speak calmly. With his stupidity coloring his face, it takes every muscle in my body not to scream at him.

I clasp my hands together. "Ky, Shelly told Rowan. Rowan then, basically, told the EN-TIRE school!"

For a while, he's silent. I don't break it. I'm done. I have nothing else to say. How could he still see her so innocently?

Well, I guess he is in love after all. His love for *her* overshadows the fact that she told Rowan.

Then, it hits me. Like a skyscraper crumbling down right on top of me.

He has a fresh haircut. His bed-tossed hair is a little shorter. He looks directly into my eyes and for the first time since I fell in love with him, I have the courage to look deep into his.

"What?" he questions.

"Are you with her?"

"He looks dumb founded. He takes his eyes off mine and looks past my shoulder. "It was bound to happen, Jo? You know how I feel about her. I couldn't bare being her friend another day."

He hangs his head like he knows or can even feel just how painful the confession is to me.

"You did this after I told you how I felt?"

Still looking at him, studying every angle of his face, every beautiful imperfection I have grown to admire.

"Yes." He looks at me with sad eyes.

All the of the air is sucked out of me. If I could look in the mirror right now, I'm sure I would look like a ghost. I gaze out at the kids running and laughing without a care in the world. I suddenly remember that light feeling. The feeling of being carefree and happy.

Happy is something I haven't felt in a long—long time.

Two words escape my lips.

"I see."

I begin to walk toward the path we took. "Don't follow me Ky."

He doesn't. It's unlike him, but I guess since he's put on his big boy pants with Shelly, he's changing right before my eyes. As I walk further and further away, I hear him faintly call out after me.

"Maybe she told Rowan so that…"

But I'm too far away to hear the rest.

Walking home, I feel weighed down, like I am treading through quicksand. I try desperately to block Kyell and his conniving girlfriend out of my head. All I want to do is get back home and start packing so I can get out of here.

My anger won't let the tears fall, but oh how I want to let every ounce of pain out on my pillow. I want to find something sharp to rid myself of it all. My breathing escalates.

It's okay. No need to get upset. There's something good that will come of this. I promise.

I want to cry out when I hear him. Adar.

Instead, I walk through the front door, pass the twins watching their Saturday morning cartoons, past my dad who is stirring paint, and up to my room. I pack within an hour—without my mom.

I don't want to talk to anyone, really, and I know that's exactly why she offered to help. I just want to get on that plane and leave all of this behind. Who knows, maybe I could stay with Grandma Ellis? Now, I just need to fall asleep so this day can end sooner.

I walk out into the hallway to grab my cell phone off my dresser. The time reads 12:31pm. The option of sleeping through the day is pretty much out. A text comes through from Ky. I ignore it and the three that follow. I check out my notifications to distract me. Dr. Brasser advised mom to delete all of my social media last year. She said it was a huge factor when it comes to my anxiety and depression. Fortunately, I was successful in talking my mom into letting me have at least one on my phone. I convinced her by telling her it's the only way I can keep up with my friends. The only reason she conceded was because she was happy, I had "friends" to keep up with.

As soon as I touch the app, I am inundated with picture after picture of me on top of Rowan—looking like a mad animal. One shows, Kyell pulling me off of her, fists bloodied, hair crazed, eyes glassed over like I'm not even there.

PSYCHO is typed across the picture in bright yellow lettering. I close the app and delete it. For good.

When the fourth text from Kyell populates in my notifications, I block him. For good.

Mick was right. I should be more careful with my heart.

23 | Sunday Morning

Mom, dad, and the twins drive me to the airport. The car ride is unusually quiet, 1). Because mom and dad had a fight just before we left the house. It was over his chosen attire for church—jeans and a button-up. He hates wearing ties outside of the courtroom, 2). Because the twins know not to speak when Mom and Dad are playing the silent game and 3). Because I have nothing to say to any of them.

When we reach the airport, I have only thirty minutes to get to my gate, which is already boarding. Mom reaches back to grab my hand before I get out of the car.

"Take care, Jo. Call me when you get there."

"Uh-huh."

I quickly touch the twins' hands, a gesture to say good-bye, hoping they won't have any problems this week.

I get out of the car quickly with Mick right on my heels. He grabs me and peers down into my eyes. "Are you okay?"

"Yeah, I'm okay." I don't look at him. He doesn't need to know I'm lying.

He hugs me tightly. "See you soon."

As I jog away, the twins yell out of the window, "See you, Friday!"

I glance back at them. They wave. I wave back.

I make it to the plane before it takes off without me, but I'm gasping for breath as I board. It's all Mom's fault. Why does it matter what Dad wears to church? The bulletin, right across the top of it, always says, "Come as You Are." Does Mom think they're bluffing or something?

My mood is brightened when I find out I have a window seat. The lavender colored sky fills me with a burst of positivity, my murky thoughts banished by the rising sun. Squeezing by a woman who looks to be around thirty and a little blonde-haired and blue-eyed boy, I make myself comfortable. I put my wireless headphones on, ready to let Adele's melodic voice sing me to sleep. Then, my phone buzzes in my bag. I pull it out, almost 100% sure it's my mom trying to apologize for making me late, but it's not.

It's a text from Zeem.

Zeem: I wish I could have seen you before you left. Why didn't you tell me you were leaving?

Jo: I'm not leaving forever...

I tell him, even though I want to.

...only for a little while

Zeem: It already feels like forever.

I don't respond. I'm too startled by the sudden quake of the plane as it speeds down the runway. The flight attendant light comes on, and the monotone bell buzzes.

"Please be sure your seatbelts are buckled, and your mobile devices are set to airplane mode..."

My thoughts are flooded with Zeem's last text, as I swipe up on my cracked screen. Just as I am about to press the little airplane icon, a text notification appears at the top of my screen.

Zeem: *Be safe. I need you back here in one piece.*

I press the button as the plane rips off into the sky. Zeem's words replay in my mind, over and over again. I can't help but feel good about him.

I first met Zeem my freshman year. He and Kyell were friends in middle school, but we had never spoken to one another until the first day of school. My mom had talked me into wearing this floral peach-colored dress that reached right above my knee, along with a small, wedged heel.

I had always worn jeans and a baggy t-shirt—never wanting to draw attention to my newly-forming upper half.

"Jo, you are a young lady now," Mom had said. "It's time you started dressing like one."

I argued with her all night and refused to step foot in that dress. The next morning, she woke me up, dress in hand, with a proposition. She said if I wore the dress, she would buy Kyell and I tickets to the concert I had been trying to save money for. Adele. It was too good to pass up. What harm could seven hours in a dress do, compared to a night with Kyell?

Mom insisted on dropping me off my first day of high school. My knees shook the entire ride to school. I guess Mom noticed. I couldn't count how many times she told me how beautiful I looked. I had to admit; the dress was pretty. It had this smooth satin finish and it slightly shimmered when just the right amount of light hit it.

I tried desperately to avoid Kyell that day. For some reason, I didn't want him to see me. I was nervous enough walking into the school, all dolled up, let alone having him lay his dark ebony eyes on me. If he looked at me, I would just melt.

When I finally made it to my first period class, AP English, my calves were on fire. Besides my eighth-grade formal, this was the only time I had ever worn anything other than flats or sneakers.

"You'll be fine," she said. "They're small wedges."

I was fuming.

Trying to walk as normal as possible, I sat down in the first desk I saw. The last row of desks, far from the front, just how I like it.

I looked to my left, and there he was. Zeem. I knew his name, but I wasn't sure if he knew mine. He caught me looking over at him and cracked a half smile.

"Hey," he said.

"Hey."

"I'm so glad to see you here," he said, turning towards me.

"Oh yeah? Why?" I couldn't bring myself to look at him.

"I hear Dr. Miles is brutal. I'm going to need a study buddy."

I smiled back at him, giving him just enough eye contact so he knew I heard him. Just then, Dr. Miles walked to the front of the room. The entire class quieted down.

I thought our little conversation was over, but it wasn't. Zeem leaned over as close as he could and whispered in my ear.

"You—look—Amazing." He said each word with emphasis in every syllable. A million little fireflies lit up in my stomach, and I never felt so seen.

That was the first day Zeem ever spoke to me. From then on, we engaged in small conversations or short texts about upcoming assignments. I was so occupied with my growing feelings for Kyell and my absent parents, I turned down every invitation to study with him.

Over the past two years, we haven't had anymore classes together. Though, we always manage to be right next to each other during lunch. He always smells so nice.

Never has he texted me as much as he has in the past few days. I'm suddenly curious. Curious to know why. My heart smiles and the vibrations of it travels up to my face.

I get this weird sensation that I'm being watched, bringing me back to reality. The little boy seated next to me is gawking up at me—smiling—like he knows my every thought. I shift all my weight to one side and face the window. Still holding my phone in my hand, I scroll through my downloads to find something that doesn't make me think of Kyell.

There isn't one song in my playlist that doesn't cause me to imagine his face. I settle on listening to Bach instrumentals. Sleep overtakes me like a violent wave.

24 | Maryland

The flight felt like an hour instead of five, thanks to my long nap. Sleep didn't come easy the night before, so I guess my exhaustion caught up with me. I feel rejuvenated when I walk out to the frigid air. I knew it still would be freezing here, so I brought a light jacket.

Silly me. I should have brought a coat.

There's actually snow on the sidewalk and the clouds seem to be telling a story of more to come. Every other traveler had gotten the memo, walking around in their snug winter wear.

I pull my jacket a little tighter around me and get a quick look at the traffic right outside of the baggage claim doors. Grandma's cobalt Buick is nowhere in sight. As soon as I pull my cell phone out, I hear a faint sound of someone calling my name from a distance.

My head pivots to scan the cars. About thirty feet away, I spot two arms waving in the air. I squint to see if it's actually her, and the silver halo floating on top of her head gives it away.

It is Grandma Ellis.

Crossing the street two cares stop to let me pass, I wave back to reassure her that I see her and I'm coming.

The weight of how long it's been knocks at my heart. And, with all the haste to get here, my safe zone is now looking a little bleak. The time we've spent not speaking is going to create quite an awkward car ride to Columbia.

"Hey, Jo!" Grandma screams.

She throws her arms around me and I welcome the warm sensation in my soul. She holds me as if I haven't been ignoring her for the past several months. She kisses my face and I feel peace set in. A peace that she wears no matter the circumstances.

Words evade me. I just hang on to her like nothing ever happened. Nothing could be more important right now than to have my very own peace capsule, all to myself.

On the twenty-mile drive to Grandma's house, a light snow fall begins. Although I hate gray skies, this Maryland sky is so reminiscent of my childhood. Filled with nostalgia, I can't help but sink down in the front seat and let it all consume me.

Spending Spring Break with Grandma was always the highlight of my school year. She'd make hot cocoa and cookies every evening. We would sit by the fireplace reading all day as we watched the snow accumulate on the windowsill.

It was always comforting to be here with her, away from all of the social angst, bullying, and unrequited love I had to deal with at home.

While reading, she would stop to tell me what was happening in her book. Grown-up people, having grown-up problems, was so interesting. It made me so eager to grow up—not to read the books, but to have a life of my own—just as exciting, of course.

I started writing when I was twelve simply because I wanted to tell Grandma Ellis a really good story during our reading time. My retellings of what I was reading, were like waiting in a doctor's office compared to the juicy gossip in the novels she read.

One day she stopped reading to clue me in on what had transpired since the day before. I was so intrigued by the story that I couldn't get to sleep that night. The way the writer held us in suspense at the end of every chapter inspired me. I stayed up and wrote my first short story before falling off to sleep.

The next evening, Grandma Ellis shared the traumatic ending to that story. I was amazed by the plot twist. Then, eager to share what I had written the night before, I asked if she would like to hear it.

"I would love to!" she'd said with wide eyes.

Thirty minutes later, I looked up at her.

I will never forget the look on her face. A look of sheer pride and joy.

It had never crossed my mind how she would react. I just wanted to share it with someone. Grandma Ellis loved the story so much she had it bound. Since then, every Christmas or birthday she buys me new stationary as one of my gifts.

The anticipation of what the new stationary will be is always unbearable. The design, the texture, and my pen running across the parchment, is a euphoria I can't begin to describe. Writing takes me to places I only dream of going and sets my world in orbit again when things seem to stop moving.

Grandma Ellis understands this about me. Sometimes I think she's the only person in the world who gets its.

"The forecast didn't call for snow," she laughs now, steering the car along the snow-speckled asphalt, "but you know the weather here is so unpredictable."

I grin along with her. "It's fine. I like it when it snows here."

"Oh, good. I can make us some hot cocoa after we get settled and you can tell me about some of the stories you've written."

Forgetting about all things Kyell, I agree, feeling more alive than I have in a long time.

❄

The snow continues to fall throughout the entire afternoon. By the time I get unpacked and Grandma finishes baking cookies, it's almost dinner time. I flop down on the plush burgundy couch next to the window and lay my head back in exhaustion.

Opening my eyes to see the large expanse of Grandma's ceiling makes me think of how many times I have done this. I swear, this couch is nothing shy of a big puffy cloud.

Minutes pass, and I can hear Grandma moving around in the kitchen.

"Do you need any help, Grandma?" My stomach growls.

"No. Just a minute. I can't find your cup."

I smile. She always serves me cocoa in a red cup with reindeer antlers on each side.

"No worries, Grandma. I'm sure the cocoa will taste just the same in a regular cup."

"Found it!" She cheers. "I'll be right there."

I glance around the familiar living room. Has anything changed? Nope. Everything is just where I left it. The room is cozy with the dim lighting and wooden accents that I love. It gives the room a sort of library vibe.

Right above the fireplace is an over-sized portrait of Mom and Mick. It's been there since I could remember. They are both dressed in the same color, champagne. Mick is wearing a bow tie with a penguin jacket, which he claims he hated, but mom insisted. He looks good, just a younger version of himself with a lot more curls and no beard.

My mom looks the same as she did so many years ago, with the exception of her new pixie cut and the growing half circles under her eyes. She's nothing short of a super model, but I've never told her.

I have always admired her in this photo. Even now, I am amazed looking at how the dress shimmers in the light, how it envelops her small frame, and how her dark wavy hair cascades down her back in big waves—I only wish I could be as pretty as her. Sometimes I get angry that she is so pretty and I'm just—oddly plain. My mom's bronze skin tone glows standing next to Mick.

She is the image of perfection. An ebony queen, someone I will never be. I'm sort of in between. Gray. Neither here nor there. Neither black nor white.

Mom is just a younger version of Grandma Ellis. She is just as beautiful. When she walks into the living area holding a full tray. I jump up to help her.

"I got it, Jo. This is good exercise," she says.

I help her anyway, getting a glimpse of her now, even more, creased face. I put my hand to her cheek. My fingers run down the side of her face. Her skin feels like a wilted rose.

She grins at me and waves my hand away. "Girl, I'm not afraid of aging. It's a sign of wisdom!" Her silvery white curls bounce around on her head when she swings her head around and puts her hand on her hip. "And this hair you're staring at is my crown."

I smile, but I know our years together are quickly running out. I can't waste any more time. My heart breaks at the thought. It doesn't matter how many secrets she tells, or how angry she makes me, while I'm here, I will act as if every day is the last day. When I get back home, I'll call her every day or maybe twice a day.

We both sit down. I grab my reindeer mug and two chocolate chip cookies. Grandma smirks with satisfaction. It gives her great joy to fill someone one to capacity. She's one of those people who will feed you until you tap out.

I give her a side glance, my head held high in confidence, "Today, I will exercise self-control and only eat when necessary."

She laughs as if she has already seen a vision of my defeat. My high hopes dissipate when I take the first bite. The cookie melts in my mouth immediately. The smooth gooey center and the crispy buttery edges cause me to drool for more. I chew slowly to savor every crispy, gooey bite.

"Are they good?" Grandma smirks.

"Are they?" I say in between bites. "They are awesome, Grandma. Thank you!"

"Now, I couldn't let you come here without baking your favorites. For dinner I've made your favorite soup and rolls."

My heart jumps with excitement. Grandma's chicken tortilla soup should be an American staple it's so delicious. She loves to cook, and I don't mind eating.

We sit for hours, chatting. I tell her about the last short story I wrote, which was several months ago. The truth is, I lost the inspiration when we had our fall-out.

She tells me about a new book she just started with her book club. She has always wanted to start a book club, but never got the nerve to actually do it. Until now, I guess.

She says it started with a few friends from church, but now there's more than fifteen women. A part of me is excited for her and another part is jealous. Excited because she is doing something she loves, retelling stories. And jealous because I'm not here to join them.

After dinner, we laugh, we cry, and then we share some more until Grandma is nodding off to sleep while I ramble on.

"Grandma." I tap her knee gently.

She jerks herself awake. "Oh, did I fall to sleep? I'm sorry, sweetie." She groans as she gets up from the couch. "Let me show you to your room."

When I was a little girl, mom and I stayed with Grandma Ellis until Mick came into the picture. They never told me why. Just like they never told me the whole story about my real dad. They always kept it simple—leaving out larger portions of the story.

It used to be enough. Now, I'm frustrated that I'm so clueless about the past.

My mom met my real dad when she was fresh out of high school. They dated off and on. Once, when they were off, mom conceived me. My mom didn't want to marry him, so they just moved in together, right before I was born. Mom says he left one night and never came back. I was about three then.

That's all I know and that's all they have allowed me to know. I can't say that I remember him. All I remember is leaning over my mom one day, while she cried for what seemed like an eternity. I peered up at this tall slender man.

His face is a blur, but his hair was as golden as straw. For years, I thought this memory was a dream, but now, I doubt it.

Walking down the hallway behind Grandma Ellis, I glimpse a photo hanging on the wall. The picture has always been there. I have probably walked past it a thousand times before. For whatever reason, the image of my mom and I is calling out to me. I'm about three in the photo, skin just as bright, with my favorite stuffed kangaroo dangling from my hands.

I stop and stand right in front of it. I stare at my twenty-something mom, her long black hair pulled back in a ponytail. She looks happy, but there's something behind the smile I can't quite grasp—an emotion that is nowhere close to happiness.

Then, I examine the younger version of myself. I'm not smiling. I've looked at this picture before, and always wondered why that stoic look was painted on my face. Did I not want to take the picture? Was I just as angry as a child as I am now?

In the past, I would just chalk it up to my mom making me take the picture. She barks out orders and I have to follow them. The usual.

But. I look at the house we are standing in front of. It's a pale green with brown shutters. It's small with only two windows. Awful. The most odd-looking house I have ever laid eyes on.

Grandma notices that I've stopped. She walks up beside me, "What's wrong, Jo?"

"I've always wondered why I'm not smiling in this picture, but mom seems to look so happy."

"Because she was. That was the day you two came to live with me."

"Why was she happy about *that?*"

"Well, she had just gotten accepted into the University of Maryland—into the nursing program. She needed the help. And," she exhales, "since, I wasn't going back to work after your grandfather died, I could be there for you 24/7."

"But why was she happy? My dad had just left her."

Grandma Ellis sucks in what seems like all the oxygen in the entire house. She lets it out slowly.

"I know, but she was happy. Tired, but happy."

Still standing side by side, looking at the familiar photo, I get the nerve. "Grandma?"

"Yes, honey."

"In a few months, I will be seventeen and I don't know anything about my real dad. I don't even know his name."

"Yes, we told you his name. It's Daniel."

"Yes, but what is his last name?"

Grandma begins to walk away. "That doesn't matter. You need to get some sleep, Jozi. We can talk about this in the morning."

"No, Grandma. I need to talk about this now. Why is this the only photo of mom when I was little?"

Grandma ignores that question and continues down the hall.

"There aren't any photos of her and I when I was baby. There are not any before this day. This is the only one. Daniel and mom dated for a long time. Why haven't I ever seen any pictures of him? Do you have any?

She doesn't even stop to look back.

"Why is talking about him so difficult for you two?"

Grandma Ellis's door shuts behind her.

"Good night!" I yell after her.

Looking at the picture one last time, I count from 20 to 1, trying to calm myself.

It doesn't work.

I drag my feet to my room, which looks just the same. I walk over to the window nook and gaze out at the snow-capped hill behind the house. The same hill I had my first kiss. I smile at the memory. Whatever was gripping my heart gently releases it and my breathing slows.

My mind is spinning, and my heart is pounding. Neither of them understands how hard it is to know nothing about your childhood or your real dad. Neither of them even cares.

I care.

My heart flutters at the sound of his voice. And just a glimmer of light flashes out at the top of the hill.

"Adar!" I whisper. "Where have you been?"

I smile wide. He walks slowly down the hill, leaving no footprints in the snow. Mystified at the reality of this moment, I almost miss when he reaches the window and walks right through it.

I'm so excited to see him, I jump up to hug him. I let go for just a second to pinch his arm. *Yep, real!* I go back to hugging him and he allows it.

Ow! He yells.

"Oh, I'm sorry!" I say quickly, holding on to the spot that's still a little red.

He begins to laugh this deep-chested laugh, and I slap the exact spot in embarrassment.

"I'm so gullible," I say, rolling my eyes.

I lay my head against his stomach, listening for a heart-beat, but before I can detect one, he escapes from my hold.

I'm a spirit, Jozi. I don't really need a heart.

"Why not? You look human."

I only look and feel this way so that you can comprehend me.

"Oh, so I won't freak out?"

Exactly. If I appeared to you in my truest form…

I don't let him finish. "Try me."

Well, not tonight. I'm here to show you something important.

I sit down on the bed, pouting. "You think I'm too sensitive to see you? Rolling my eyes, I reply, "Important? Okay."

He looks down at me. His eyes are firmly trained on mine. In an instant, they light up like white laser beams. Shards of light bolt out of his eyes straight into mine.

25 | Nicole

Once you've gone numb, being hurt by someone is pretty much impossible. It's like you have created this false universe that only specified people are allowed to gain access.

For me, that was Kyell. Besides him, I never fathomed I would ever feel anything again. Now, here I am sitting in a very familiar room that—get this—my guardian angel, who I actually believe is real now, transported me to! A room that causes a windstorm of emotions to blow right through me.

I'm a little shaken up by the whole trip here, but I feel at home. The room is blue and white with one small window. The blinds are awkwardly drawn, and the room is quaint and quiet.

Then, from out of nowhere, a little girl with golden yellow pig tails scurries into the room and shuts the door. Her chest heaves in and out and her face is soaked. She darts to the farthest corner from the door and cowers. With er knees pulled up to her chest and her head down she sniffles quietly.

I know her.

Her small round head. Pink fingers clenched around her arms. She's me. She's a three-year-old version of me.

I slowly walk toward her, feeling every painful whimper she lets escape. I advance closer, hoping I can sooth her, but I'm jolted by the piercing scream from out in the hallway. I look at Adar, who is standing near the door. He tilts his head toward it.

I shake my head no, afraid of what I might see.

You asked why.

I look back at the little version of myself. Is this real? Did this really happen?

It all comes back in a fog. Slowly, I walk towards the door. The screams are getting louder, and the walls begin to quake from the impact of whatever is happening on the other side of that door.

I hear a man's voice. When I open the door to peek my head out, my heart begins to pound like a jackhammer over what I think I might see.

They can't see you, Jozi. Don't be afraid. Besides, I'm here.

His eyes reassure me. I take a deep breath and take another step forward.

My mom is pinned up against a wall in the hallway by a man—a tall, slender man with blonde hair. She squirms under his two hands squeezed tightly around her neck.

"So, what did you say you were going to do?" The man speaks with gritted teeth. "Did you say you were leaving?"

He pulls back, leaving one hand around her neck and uses the other to slap the wind out of her. Mom collapses to the floor. I run to her limp body. Her face is purple and bulging with blood dripping from her nose and mouth. I fletch at the sight of her then I am thrown into to action to protect her, but it's no use. This has already happened. There's nothing I can do.

The monster standing over me begins to laugh, "Get up! You're not dead." He demands, Get up!"

He kicks her to see if she moves. She doesn't.

Tears pour as rage boils over inside of me. My fists crack as I flex my hands ready to lay into his face every ounce of depression, anxiety, and anger I have lurking inside of me. Standing to my feet, I face him. Then, there, in his raged filled eyes, I see something.

I see—*me.*

He's my father. I examine his face, his hair, his lips, his nose, all mine. A million thoughts race through my mind and I am transfixed.

He kneels over my mom. "Wake up, Nikki," he cries out. "Come on, wake up!"

She doesn't. For all I know, she might have been holding her breath, but with the look of death covering her, my heart stops. I, for a moment, think she is dead.

Like one of those bad dreams you try to wake up from and then you realize it's not real.

Thank God, it's not real.

She lived.

I lived.

He stumbles to his feet, gasping for breath. Spinning in a circle, obviously disoriented, he moves quickly down the hall. He grabs what sounds like a set of keys. The front door slams shut and seconds letter I hear an engine roar. Like a coward, he leaves my half-dead mother on the floor without a second glance.

And me! What about his three-year-old terrified daughter in the bedroom? As rage continues to knock, I hear a car's tires spin. Shaking, I kneel down next to my mom and hold her.

"I see why you kept me from him, now. I see. I'm sorry, momma. I'm so sorry."

Moments pass, small footsteps run up the hallway. I jump at the sound, ready to defend my mom, but it's me—little, three-year-old me. The young me slowly walks up to my mom's body and begins to shake her.

"Mommy," I say in between breaths "Mommy, wake up."

She does. Very easily she falls onto her back like she has been awake this entire time. Slowly, she sits up. "Is he gone, Jo?"

"Yes, daddy—left."

She wraps her arms around me. "Oh, good. Thank God he's gone. You did good sweet heart. Thank you for doing what mommy said."

As she stands to her feet, blood drips from her face into little Jozi's hair, staining my pale golden curls. Mom notices and at the sight of this she breaks down. She sobs her way back down to the floor—curling her body into a fetal position.

Little me, unaware of what just happened, lays over my mom's back.

"Don't cry, Mommy. Don't cry."

The entire memory of my father comes flooding back like fragments of a broken mirror being put back together again. This is the memory that was erased. This memory is truth. This memory is the day *I* decided to forget. The memory I locked away.

26 | Letting Go

The next morning, I wake up not remembering how I made it back to my bed, let alone this part of the timeline. Adar is, as usual, not around to silence the chaos in my head after one of our little field trips.

I sit up to try to gain some normalcy. The sun is shining outside my window, but I can still see sharp icicles hanging down from the roof. I stumble out of bed to get my house coat and realize I am still wearing yesterday's clothes. I groan in disgust, then hop in the shower.

While I finish washing up, I can hear Grandma probing around in the kitchen. I guess I'll go and help and even try to make amends about last night. When I head down the hallway, that same photo catches my attention again. I look at my face, then at my mom's. Now I see it. Now I understand my stoic look. I was traumatized and didn't even know it. Looking at the picture now, I can even see the discoloration of the right side of my mom's face.

My mouth drops open. All this time and I never stopped long enough to notice what was right in front of me. Dr. Brasser has never missed an opportunity to tell me that "Trauma can sometimes cause you to push away or forget painful memories." I never understood why she would say this so often. I never cared till now.

"Good morning!" Grandma calls down the hallway.

"Good morning, Grandma," I reply, startled back to reality.

I walk into the kitchen and take a seat at the breakfast bar. It smells like Grandma is baking again, but I can't quite make out what I'm smelling. It smells sweet and savory at the same time.

"What are you cooking?"

"Oh, just some good old-fashion French toast and I have some turkey bacon in the oven."

"Umm, smells good."

She looks at me from over her shoulder, "So, how did you sleep?"

I think to tell her about my little escapade last night, but it's too risky. They already think I'm crazy. Why give them more reasons to continue sending me to Dr. Brasser? Instead, I go about it another way.

"Grandma?"

"Yes." She sighs, giving the French toast a flip.

"I remember."

She slowly presses the spatula against the French toast one last time before she scoops it out of the pan. She doesn't reply.

"I remember the day my real dad left."

She brings the food over to the counter without making eye contact.

"Grandma, did you hear me? I remember that day."

Sitting down next to me, she asks, "Why didn't you tell us?"

"The memory of it just came back to me—last night. I was so angry that you left me out in the hallway with no answers, I just…"

"Listen, Jo. Your mom and I worked really hard to shield you from the trauma of the first three years of your life. When that part of your life was over, there was no point in bring it up or talking about it."

"I know, but didn't you think I would ask about him some day? I mean—"

"Yes, but you have Mick. Mick came into you and your mom's life at the perfect time."

She's right, my Grandpa had just left—well, passed away, but I thought he had left too. At that age I had no idea what death meant. I can't remember how I felt, if anything. But did know two men had left me suddenly and around the same time. Maybe that could have been the reason I suppressed the memory of it all.

Wow. Dr. Brasser and I will have a lot to talk about next week.

I ask a critical question, since she seems to be open to talking now.

"Have you guys ever heard from him since that day? Like, has he tried to find me?"

Grandma gives me the look. The look that says I'm pushing it.

"Your momma will have a fit if she finds out I'm talking to you about this."

"Grandma, please." I grab her hand. "I have to know. I promise to never look for him, but..."

I hang my head. A flash of his familiar face comes back.

"I have to know if he ever looked for me."

She squeezes my hand. "He did. A few months after he left, he came back to the house—banging on the door and windows. We asked the neighbors to keep a look out for him. You two weren't there, though. You were staying with me.

He called your mom constantly until she had to take out a restraining order. He claimed that he was sorry—that when he had beat your mom half to death, he got spooked and ran because he thought she was dead. He said he regretted everything."

She paused, wiping tears away. Hearing this from her, finally, was tormenting. But I couldn't get emotional. Not now. I need to know the whole story, and breaking down now will only prove how fragile I am. I have to appear strong.

I rub her back. "Go on, Grandma."

"Your mom needed a strong lawyer to get full custody of you. That's how she met Mick. She insisted on not revealing the beatings to the court. She wanted to win without shaming him, but the truth came out just like I knew it would.

She looks up at me, knowing the shock she would see. I had no idea that Mick ever set eyes on my real dad, let alone defended my mom in a court case about *me*.

I play it cool, but inside I'm fuming about the walls of secrets they have built around me. They didn't lie about how they met, but it wasn't technically the whole truth either.

"When your mom got full custody, Daniel was enraged. He threatened to kill her. Nicole didn't feel safe. She stayed in the house for weeks. Mick tried getting her to come out just to go to the store. Her psychiatrist had to meet with her here at the house because she wouldn't even go to her sessions. It was a pretty penny when it was all said and done.

Grandma Ellis sighed, rubbing her forehead.

"I was a mess. I felt powerless. Then, a miracle happened. Well, it may seem like something horrible to other people, but for us, it was a work of God."

She stops. She looks up at me like she's finished. Like she thinks she may have gone too far.

"Grandma, there's nothing you can say that will surprise me at this point. I promise."

"I know. I just feel like I'm betraying Nicole. She should have been the one to tell you all of this stuff—not me." She hangs her head once again.

"Yeah, but I don't think she ever would have, Grandma. She's like a stone wall. So, I need you to tell me." I gently lift her head, so our eyes meet.

"You know, you always tell me that God has a plan—that everything happens for a reason. I believe me being here is part of His plan. It's like after everything that I have been through, this is the climax, or I guess you can say the resolution of this chapter of my life. I'm ready to move on Grandma, but I can't until I know what those missing pieces are."

Unaware of the walls that I have just let down, tears start to flow. I quickly wipe them away almost startled at how quickly they have come.

"Continue, Grandma. Please."

All of the sudden, our roles switch and she begins to rub circles on my back, causing even more tears to fall.

"Okay, sweetheart. You're right." She exhales deeply. "The miracle that we didn't expect was his arrest. Daniel had always been involved in drugs, but Nicole just refused to see it. When Mick found out about the case, he came straight to the house to let us know."

Grandma Ellis shrugged. "Daniel was convicted of drug possession with intent to distribute. He got three years for it, but it was enough time for your mom and Mick to fall in love and get married. Mick was such a rock for Nicole during that time, shoot, I told her she better not let him go."

She laughs at the memory, her eyes far away.

"Of course, she was hesitant with all that she had been through. Mick decided to change the course of his law career and go after the big cases, so he did. When it was close to the time for Daniel to be released, things became strained for all of us. Even Mick seemed a little off kilter. You, on the other hand, were the happiest little girl. By this time, you were six and Daniel had become a faint memory. Mick got an offer for a position in Seattle and you all moved there just before Daniel's release."

"Did he ever come around looking for us?"

"Yeah, he called a few times. He sounded so—I don't know. Empty. Anyway, I told him you all were gone and warned him that if he called or even set foot on my property, I would press charges for harassment. I haven't heard from him since. Though, a few years after that, I heard he was arrested again for beating some poor woman to death."

Grandma continues to rub my back as I wipe the tears away. "You know what Grandma, I'm glad you all kept this from me this long."

"Why do you say that?"

I look at her and smile through the pain. "Because this is a really sad—sad story!"

We both laugh through our tears and spend the rest of the morning catching up. I can tell that she feels lighter and free. She never laughed so loud.

On the outside, I laugh right along with her. On the outside, I joke just to make her feel better about what she has shared, inside, there's still this unsettled feeling of some kind. I should feel free and resolute, but there's this feeling. A feeling you get when something good has happened, but you get distracted by something else. It lingers there in the dark corners of your mind, lobbying for your attention, but you push through to appear normal, because you have no idea what it is.

Am I angry at Daniel for what he did to my mom and I; angry at all of them for keeping this from me so long? Do I feel guilt? Sadness? And for who? Who am I feeling this for—my mom, Daniel, or myself?

I don't have the answers, just more confused emotions.

When night falls, I go to my room. Exhausted from the show I put on for Grandma all day. I don't want her to feel like it is her fault that I feel this way, so I keep the act up all day. I pretend to be happy and free from the secrets too.

I walk into the room and shut the door behind me. Standing there, staring into space, solemn and still, I hear something, but I don't allow it to distract me from my stare. There in the center of the most peaceful place in the universe, deep inside my mind is chaos. I stare so hard my eyes cross and I have to blink them back into position.

I hear it again. A steady rhythm of something hitting a wooden surface. The melodic sound has been continuous since I walked into the room. The sound of it has actually calmed me and, as I stand here in a daze, I welcome it.

You are okay.

"You think so?"

I know so. If I knew that this would make things worse for you, I would not have shown you your past.

"You know, I figured it was you, coming to distract me from myself. But that hasn't seemed to work out all that well, Adar. You see the more you show me the worse off I am. This only causes me to see myself as more tattered and bruised."

And that's the problem, Jozi.

"I know that, Adar! Don't you think I know that! I just can't help it if I'm constantly reminded of how horrible I really am. I mean, all this time I couldn't even see the hero my mom really is or the savior Mick was and still is to our family!"

I crumple to the floor, dizzy from the charged emotions spilling over out of me.

No, Jozi. Get up. You are not going to make this about you again.

I grunt and push against the floor, just hard enough for my knuckles to turn pink and I ignore him.

This isn't about you realizing how horrible you are. This is about you placing your attention on someone other than yourself. You see, when you focus on others and how messed up their life is your problems don't seem so gigantic. They get smaller.

I sit up, feeling pure exhaustion. I don't' even turn to look at him.

"I don't have a clue what you're talking about. Just leave me alone."

You will. Don't worry.

You will.

27 | Six More Days

It's Tuesday. The lush white snow has turned into rough ice patches revealing the dead grass here and there. Grandma Ellis knocks at my door, almost singing "Good Morning."

I would have chosen to remain asleep and not have woken up at all, but I am grateful to hear her happiness. She invites me out to a spontaneous trip to New York. I conjure up the perfect lie and tell her I started my period.

Miraculously, she believes me. She cooks me breakfast and then heads out by herself. I've never known her to wait around on anybody. A four- hour drive to New York would seem like an eternity to any other sixty-five-year-old, especially without someone to switch out the responsibility of driving.

But it's Grandma Ellis. She doesn't let anything—or anyone—stop her. I guess that's where my mom gets it from.

I sit around watching morning shows and the news, every now and again replaying Adar's words.

This isn't about you realizing how horrible you are. This is about you placing your attention on someone other than yourself.

Yep, that's how he sees me. That's how everyone sees me. Spoiled and self-centered. Even Kyell said so.

Jozi Skies is not only an over-reacting spoil brat, but she is also selfish. Yep, I'm selfish. All I think about is myself and how everyone treats me. Can't anyone see how messed up *my* life is?

When is someone going to stop and notice!

My phone buzzes on the counter in the kitchen where I left it. I get tangled up in my blanket, feeling a sudden urgency.

I have three missed calls and one new text message. Two calls are from my mom and one is from Mick. I ignore them and check my text from Zeem, first. Maybe he has something nice to say.

How's the weather in MD.

Jozi: Cold

Zeem: How are you?

I lie.

Jozi: Super!

Zeem: Don't you know that I am used to your sarcasm, by now? And why the one word answers?

I don't respond. Okay, so I guess I am also a pessimistic liar.

Zeem: Do you want to talk about it?

Jozi: NOPE. How are you?

Zeem: Okay. Well, I'm good. But…

Jozi: But what?

Zeem: I would be doing better if I could see you.

I blush at the thought that, Zeem, the quiet cutie at lunch, the one person that has ever told me that I look "amazing," wants to see me. I lay back on the couch. What do I say? He texts again.

Zeem: Can I video message you.

What?

Jozi: *No! Aren't you in school?*

Zeem: *Not technically.*

I rush to the bathroom to wipe the sleep from my face. I redo the big messy bun sitting on top of my head. Am I really going to do this? I put on some Chapstick and double-check my face. I'm so pale. I pinch my cheeks to give them some color, but nothing improves the hot mess staring back at me.

Zeem: *Come on, Jo. I promise, you always look good to me.*

Okay. Why not?

Jozi: *Call me.*

Within seconds, my face appears on my phone like I'm looking into a mirror. My breath catches. I can't breathe. Why is he calling me? Why did I agree to this?

I take a deep breath in and exhale it out. I press the bright green button.

His handsome face fills the screen.

"What's up, Jo!" He gives me the biggest smile, I swear I can see all of his teeth. It's the best smile I have seen in a while.

"Oh, nothing much." I blush right back at him.

Just—you know, discovering my awful, traumatic past.

He must be at a meet or something because he's outside and it sounds like he's surrounded by hundreds of people.

"Where are you?"

"We are at our first track meet for the season—remember, March 25th?"

"Oh yeah, sorry. I've just been trying really hard not to think about school."

Wait. That means Kyell is there too. I wonder for a split second if he is nearby. I brush it off.

"I know. That's a good thing. Keep it up, but just try to fit me into some of those thoughts. Maybe that will help." He smiles, looking straight into my eyes. "I miss my friend. Lunch is so boring without you."

There, in his eyes, I can see what he says is genuine. I wish I could say I have missed him too, but to tell the truth I haven't had time to even think about him since the last text he sent me.

So, I don't.

He looks down, and I can almost see his disappointment, but he recovers quickly.

"Well, I don't want to keep you long. I just wanted to see your face."

From the background I hear someone shouting. "Hey! Who are you talking to?"

Suddenly, Chadwick's goofy face appears from over Zeem's shoulder. "Oh hey, Skies."

"Hey, Chad." I give him a half smile.

He jabs Zeem in the shoulder. "You better hurry and get off the phone with your girl friend before Coach catches you."

Zeem smiles, never taking his eyes off me. Right behind Chad comes Kyell. He laughs unknowingly and stops in mid stride. "Oh—hey, Jo. What…I've been trying…"

Chad pulls him away before he can finish, but he looks so dumbfounded I don't think he would have gotten the rest of the sentence out anyway.

I smile right back a Zeem, grateful for his video call. "Well, you better get going."

"Yeah." He looks over his shoulder coming back to reality. "Thank you for gracing my screen with your beautiful face." He smiles really big once more.

I smile back. "No problem. Call me later?"

"Okay! He perks up at the thought. "I will!"

Zeem winks, then the side of his mouth curls up into a smile so sincere it fills my heart.

We hang up.

At this point I am beyond blushing. I pick up one of Grandma's plush pillows and squeeze it close to me, almost wanting to yelp.

Then, Kyell finds his way back into my thoughts. I wonder if he heard Chad call me Zeem's girlfriend? I wonder if he believes it. A week ago, I told him I love him.

I shove the thought away. It's not like he cares—I mean, he's Shelly's now.

⁂

Most of my day is taken up with thoughts of, Zeem. His smooth cocoa skin. The way his eyes danced when I answered. His saddened expression when I didn't tell him I missed him.

Around lunch time, I begin to miss Grandma Ellis. I spend about an hour studying angels because all the good morning shows have ended. One thing I discover about them is that they were always commonplace in biblical days. In every scripture I read, I find that no one ever seemed surprised—frightened, yes, but never surprised when they appeared.

When an angel appeared, they just appeared from nowhere. It was as if people back then believed in their existence so much that it didn't move them to the point of fainting or hysteria. Take Mary, the mother of Jesus. She didn't flinch when Gabriel showed up telling her she would become pregnant before she even got married.

This story left me dumbfounded. Her reaction was accepting and poised. Why? I think about when I first met Adar. It all leads me to be a little more skeptical of these scriptures, but a part of me feels like I have to accept them. Otherwise, this would mean that Adar *is* a figure of my imagination.

But, he's not. He's more real than anything I have experienced before.

In the afternoon I call mom even though I know she might not pick up. She's at work and she never answers her phone for me when she's at work. As I am dialing the number, I decide to leave her a message for once, but surprisingly, she answers.

"Hey, Jo!"

"Hi, Mom, how are you?"

I can hear the murmurs of people's voices and the beeping of hospital machines filling the space around her.

"I'm good. How is everything going with you?"

"Great! Grandma took off to New York this morning. I didn't want to go, so she went by herself. You know how she is—when she sets her mind on something, she executes."

Mom laughs. "Yeah, she is a busy-body that one."

"You are one to talk. I'd forgotten how much alike you two are."

"Oh hush, Jozi. You are a busy-body, too. You just haven't slowed down enough to realize it yet."

I laugh and several seconds pass before either of us say anything. What's she thinking. I get a sudden urge to tell her, "I remember," but I don't.

"Mom?"

"What's up?"

"Can I ask you something?"

She hesitates. "Yeah. Sure."

"Why do you work so hard? I mean—why do you spend so much time at the hospital?"

"Well, that's easy. I thought you were going to ask something else."

"Like what?"

"It doesn't matter. The short answer to your question is—sometimes—when I think about all we have and what it took to get it, a huge chasm of fear opens up inside of me. I think about how I don't want you girls to ever want for anything."

"But, Mom, what about Mick? He provides for us."

"Right, but I don't want you ever thinking that you have to depend on a man to take care of you. Jozi, you don't need to make a boy the center of your universe to feel complete or whole. Have a plan B. You can find happiness by yourself. I want you girls to know that. I have always made it a point to show you girls that it is possible. You can survive without a man. Do you hear me, Jo?"

"What do you mean by a 'plan B?'"

"A plan just in case things don't work out."

And just like that, it's all crystal clear. I had never thought about it because I never knew the whole story about her and Daniel. Now I know why she stayed with him all that time. I force unruly tears back.

"Okay, Mom. I won't."

"I love Mick. He's a good man. I have never doubted that he would do just as he promised, but I realized a long time ago that I didn't want my girls making the same mistakes I made."

"And what was that, Mom?"

"Putting all of my focus on having a companion, so much so I lost myself. Whatever you do, Jozi, don't lose yourself for anyone else."

"Nurse, Skies, you are needed at the front desk. Nurse, Skies, you are needed at the front desk."

"Okay, Jo, I'm being summoned. Have fun with Momma. I will see you Friday."

"I love you, Mom."

"Love you too. Bye."

"Bye."

Around seven that night, Grandma comes stumbling in with her arms full of bags. I knew she was up to something. I run to help her as she collapses on the couch.

"What's all this, Grandma?"

"Oh, some of it is clothes for me." She giggles. "But I had to go to this little shop in the heart of New York City to get something for you." She smiles with an oddly sneaky expression.

I begin rummaging through the bags. "Like what, Grandma? You drove all the way to New York for what?"

Then, I see them! My once-melancholy demeanor is banished, and I cannot contain my excitement. I look over at her, grinning with a smile that is almost painful.

"Grandma, you didn't!"

I pull out six beautifully colored Moleskin luxury stationary pads. I trace my fingers over the embossed brand on the front. *Blan-Catia.*

"Do you remember the last time we went to New York?" she asks.

Last summer, before she discovered my secret, Grandma took us all to New York. We'd never been before, and the twins really wanted to see the Statue of Liberty. I wanted to visit the famous Balthazar restaurant instead. As usual, I was outnumbered, and I had to do what they wanted. We took a ferry and—although I was in a sour mood at the beginning—I ended up loving it.

It felt like I was in a story-book, living out the life of a character who has always wanted to visit New York City, and finally, after making the trip out to be a tiresome chore for most of the day, I decided to live in the moment.

Afterward, we toured the most famous streets—Broadway, 5th Avenue, Bleecker Street—for shopping and saw everything I had only seen on television. When we came upon a little shop full of books and stationery, I just had to go inside. The twins were bored after ten minutes in the shop, but I was enchanted. I could stay there the entire day and never get hungry or tired.

I paused when I saw the shelf full of luxury stationary made by some company called *Blan-Catia*. They were moleskin note pads of every color decorating the shelf. Slowly picking up a navy-blue pad, I'd ran my fingers over the smooth cover. The stationery on the inside was a delicate linen texture with stained edges—each pad having the correlating stained colored edges as the cover. I wanted one in every color, but the pads were sixty dollars apiece.

Grandma had already spent so much money that day, I didn't bother lingering at the table any longer. I didn't know she had noticed how fascinated I was, but I guess she did.

I hold all six, each a different dark shade of the rainbow to my chest, like I just found a hidden treasure.

"Grandma, *six*! You bought me six of them!"

She points to the flat bag that has a box in it, "And I brought you back some pizza from that place you wanted to visit last time—what's it called…"

I squeal with excitement, and I run over and jump on her lap. She groans, but she welcomes my attack with a warm hug.

"You are definitely, the best Grandma, EVER!"

As I smooch her delicate cheek in gratitude, I rid my mind of the selfish thoughts from earlier. I guess, my life isn't all that messed up. Someone sees me.

28 | Not Today

Last night, I wrote for hours. I was so inspired by Grandma's gift I started a new short story. It was starting to get really good, when Zeem texted me. I spent the rest of the night on facetime with him. We talked about track most of the time because he knew school was off limits. When we got tired of talking about track, I talked about my writing. He begged me to read him some of my stories, so I did. It was awkward sharing something so personal, but in a way extremely therapeutic considering what I went through the day before.

I wake up around 2 a.m. with a dead phone in my hands. I'd fallen asleep! The only question is, who fell asleep first?

I cringe at the thought of it being me. I lay in bed unwilling to face the cold draft in my room. I flop over on to my stomach and tuck my arms underneath me to trap some of the warmth. Grandma must have turned the heater off. I'm freezing.

I hear steps quickly coming up the hallway. "Grandma?"

My door bursts open. Grandma's face is creased with worry.

"Jozi, you have to get up. We have to go."

She staggers into the room and begins gathering my things, in a rush, putting them into my suitcase.

I jump at the panic in her voice and the haste in her steps.

"What is it? What's wrong?"

"We have to get back to Seattle."

I still have two more days here, two more relaxing days. "What do you mean we have to get back?"

"I am coming with you."

"Grandma, what's going on!"

"Just hurry, Jo. We don't have time to discuss this now." Tears are in her eyes and her hands are shaking uncontrollably. "I will tell you all about it when we make it to that plane."

I grab her hands. "What is going on, Grandma?"

She looks at me with complete terror in her eyes. "Mick has been shot."

⁕⁂⁕

Walking through those glass hospital doors, everything seems to move in slow motion. I see faces, but I can't hear any voices. My heartbeat has slowed, and my breath is stuck in my chest, but I will my feet to move.

When I make it to the ICU, everyone seems to be motionless. Mick's room is right in the center of the hallway. The entire wall is made out of clear plexiglass. There's no room for my imagination, I can see everything that is happening in that room. My eyes focus in on Mick. Doctors and nurses are surrounding his bed and I can't see his face, but I know it's him. His hand is hanging slightly off the bed.

The same hand that would cup the back of my head whenever he kissed my cheek when he got home from work. The same hand that has a heart shaped birthmark. The same birthmark that he told me was tattooed there personally by

God. A reminder to him why he was put on the earth—to love me. When the twins came along the story included them.

I gather the courage to walk across the threshold. Noticing no one familiar, I focus on getting to him, to his hand. Why hasn't anyone noticed his hand is hanging off the bed. Someone needs put it on the bed. Arms and hands pull me in the opposite direction. I push against the bodies, limbs tugging at me. I get close enough to see his chest slowly moving up and down, covered with wires. His nose has two tiny tubes in each nostril. A fat tube is stuck down his throat. His eyes are closed. Why are his eyes closed?

I break away for the arms and hands, running closer to the glass window that separates us. I glance around the room and my eyes meet my mom's. Her eyes are strained and red, her face swollen.

"Mom!"

She jumps up from the chair as I am being carried away. When she finally reaches me, I am in a small waiting room. Alone. She rushes into the room, bringing with her all the once muted, sounds of the hospital.

She falls into my lap, sobbing, "Jo! Oh, Jo!"

I don't know what to do, or what to say. One hand finds its way to her shoulder and squeezes it gently. We sit there for what seems like hours. No one speaks. No one moves. No one ever comes to check on us. I sit there—numb—despondent—motionless.

Mom seems to have fallen asleep, so I reach over to grab the television remote. Up in the right corner of the small and artic room is a television. I turn it on to see a young, male news reporter, standing right outside the hospital.

Today, defense attorney, Mick Skies was shot down in broad daylight while at a local home improvement store. Sources say that Mr. Skies was the defense attorney in a case against Terrance Viper, whom Skies helped to convict just last month. Viper's longtime girlfriend, and mother of his son, testified against him in the case and was tragically killed just weeks after the conviction. Could these two shootings be related? Could we have a second murder on our hands? Only time will...

I turn it off, regretting I even turned it on in the first place. Mom stirs and then

shoots up from my lap.

"Mick!" She cries out.

"Mom, it's me, Jo." I tap her shoulder.

"Where's Mick? Where's the twins?"

Her eyes are just as puffy and red as they were before. I pat down her frizzed head of hair. She puts both hands up to her head, as if to block out the recollection of where she is.

"I thought it was a dream. I hoped it was a dream." She stands to her feet frantically. "I have to go check on Mick. Are you okay, alone? I will come back to get you as soon as I can. You know, to tell you what happened."

Then she leaves. She doesn't wait for a response—she just leaves. It's okay, though. I understand. The same awful thoughts going through my head are probably even darker in hers.

I sit in a welcomed silence for almost a minute before Grandma enters the room. She looks surprisingly calm. There's no evidence of tears, but the worry strategically hidden behind her eyes.

"Did your mom tell you?" She slowly sits down next to me.

"No, she just slept."

"Oh."

"But, I know. Channel 12 told me."

"Oh."

More silence.

"Are you okay?" She rubs my hand. "You know everything is going to be okay, right?"

I snatch my hand away. "And how do you know that, Grandma?"

"Because God is in control."

"And why, if He is in such great control, did He allow this to happen!"

She gazes down at her now clasped hands.

"Exactly!" I jump to my feet. "Just what I thought. No one can figure Him out, Grandma. I don't understand why He allows things like this to happen."

She pulls me back down to the chair. "Sit down honey. Please."

"No, Grandma. Not today. My dad cannot die today. This is too soon. It wasn't enough time. Not today, Grandma. Not today." I sit down, sobbing on her shoulder.

"Oh, honey." She gives way to the tears she has been holding back. "Mick is going to die, but not today, and definitely not soon. Don't think like that. Just pray. Come on," she wipes several tears away, drying her hands on her jeans, "Let's pray together."

She grabs my hands and I reluctantly takes hers.

"Father God…"

She begins, and I just go numb again. I can't hear what she's asking for, but I don't need to hear it. I already know.

I have heard prayers like this so many times in my life that I probably could recite every word.

Sometimes the prayers would prove to be successful—or answered, if you will—, but more often those prayers are answered with silence. How do we know this prayer will be one of the answered ones? How do we know what He will decide to do?

Grandma finishes with, "In Jesus' name. Amen."

She looks at me and repeats, or I guess asks, "Amen?"

With complete doubt, I respond, "Amen."

She straightens her frame and looks over at the now-gray television screen.

"You know, Jo. You are right. We will never be capable of figuring everything out about God. Even when we get to heaven, there will be thousands upon thousands of things we will still not know about Him. But, there's one thing we know that will answer every question about Him. This one thing reveals aspects of Him that settles us, strengthens us, and complete us."

Anger toward God brews inside of me, that anger threatening every glimmer of light that I have left.

"What is it?"

She looks over at me, with fresh tears in her eyes.

"He is *good,* Jozi. God is absolute goodness. So, no matter what you face in life or how bad things get, remember, He is only good and everything that He is a part of *is good.*"

"Well, if He's so good, why would he allow this to happen?"

"Honey, God had nothing to do with this. Evil entered into the world so long ago and has been here ever since."

I throw my hands up.

"That still doesn't answer my question, Grandma."

"God is in control, Jo. Even though evil did this to Mick, God will make it work out for Mick's good."

Shaking my head, I don't respond. I don't understand.

She wraps her arms around me. "Just wait. You'll see. He has never failed me yet."

We stayed in the hospital that night. I was allowed to go in to sit with Mick for a little while. Talking to him without a reply was awkward, but I kept talking because mom said the doctors said it's good for him.

Mom won't tell me everything the doctors are saying. I have seen enough drama series to know what this all means. I'm not stupid. Mick is probably in a coma or has all of those machines breathing for him. Talking to him helps him to know that we are here. It keeps his brain active.

So, I talk. No matter how stupid I feel or no matter how silly what I'm talking about sounds, I talk until my throat feels like I've swallowed sand.

When Mrs. Cravic comes to visit the next morning, she offers to take me home to take a shower. I ask about the twins for the first time since I've been back. She lets me know they are okay. A small piece of me has missed them, so I get up, stretching as my joints pop and adjust to this foreign thing called standing. Mom, who is over on the opposite side of the room, asleep, sits up quickly, like someone called her name.

"Are you leaving, Jo? Where's Momma?"

"Yes, but I'll be back. Grandma went down stairs to get coffee." I walk over to her and begin rubbing down stray strands of her hair. I have never seen her like this—wrinkled clothes, messy hair, no make-up. It's kind of scary.

She looks over at Mick and her eyes begin to well up with tears all over again.

"He's still not awake," she says.

I walk over to the side of the bed. Mick's hair is still perfectly moussed and, even with all that he's been through, he still looks handsome and peaceful. Slowly lifting my hand to touch his hair, I hesitate and back away. Mrs. Cravic touches my arm.

"It's okay, Jo. You can touch him."

"No. I don't want to."

I turn around to face them. Mrs. Cravic fidgets with her purse looking as though she wants to say something, but she doesn't. I look down at Mom who hasn't changed her stare since she's sat up, the tears still stuck in the wells of her eyes.

"Mom, don't you want to go home to shower?"

"No, I'm fine here. The hospital has a shower I can use."

"But, don't you want to change clothes?"

"There's a change of clothes in my locker." The tears finally start to fall.

"Okay, mom." I touch her shoulder, "I'll be back."

She grabs my wrist. "Jo?" She doesn't look at me.

"Yes, mom?"

"You remember what I told you the other day, you know about having a plan B?"

"Uh, yeah. I remember."

"Well, I don't." She looks at me with a saturated face. "I don't have a plan B. And—I don't want one."

She releases my arm, then hangs her head. I bend down to kiss her cheek.

"Don't worry, Mom, I know what you meant."

She nods. "Good."

"I will be back, okay?"

When we arrive at my house, I can't even remember getting in the car or the drive here. Everything is a blur and if Mrs. Cravic said anything, I didn't hear it. All I can think about is the devastating thoughts my mom is replaying in her mind. I know Grandma Ellis is the right person to be there with her, because I can't help her. I'm a dam ready to break at any moment.

The twins run down the stairs, full of questions, when I come through the door. They hug me tight and I return it with a tight squeeze of my own.

"Is Dad awake? Where's mom? Are we going to go back? Where's Grandma?"

I take a deep breath in, "No, Dad isn't awake. Mom is still there. We are going back this afternoon and Grandma is going to keep Mom company."

They recoil and just stand there, staring at me as if I can fix this mess. I can't and I'm angry that I can't fix it for them, for mom, for Mick, for me. I dismiss the thoughts quickly before they boil over out of me.

Starting up the stairs, I yell backdown, "I'm going to shower. I will be down in a little while."

When I get to the top of the stairs, I'm met with all of my furniture that I moved into the hallway before I left. With all the excitement of visiting Grandma, and getting away from Kyell, I had forgotten about my room. I exhale—preparing my mind to deal with the mess I have to face on the other side of the door, Slowly, I push open the door. Unexpectedly, I am met with the wind, the sky, sun, moon, and stars. All at once, sweeping from one side of my room to the next, in brilliant white, blues, and yellows are the elements that make up the heavens. It all takes my breath away. Awestruck, I walk in and do a 360 to take in what I am seeing. A *Starry Night.*

"Dad, thought you would love it." Hazel says behind me. "He knows how you love that painting. He was at the department store getting something to finish it up."

My head drops. "Please give me some time alone, Hazel."

Hazel backs out of the way as I shut the door. The room begins to spin.

He was at the department store because of me.

I floor falls beneath me. On the cold, wooden surface I pour out all of my anger, devastation, and confusion. I cry until all of my pride is converted into a huge puddle of tears. The only words I can articulate come out in a small, humbled whisper.

Please don't let him die, God… please.

29 | Four More Days

When I was younger, I remember going through fits of anxiety because I couldn't shake the thought my parents dying. I didn't want to go to school because I would think, "What if this is the last day I will ever see them?" What if my mom gets in a car accident?" What if my dad catches a bad disease?"

I would pretend to be sick just to stay home and when they caught on to my tricks and sent me to school anyway, I would pretend to be sick so they would pick me up. I don't remember when I stopped having anxiety attacks about losing my parents. Maybe it was when my life became more about friends, boys, social media.

I don't know where the anxiety about my parent's well-being has been hiding all of this time, but it's back with a vengeance. My chest is tight, and my thoughts are scrambled. Trying to focus on one simple thought is difficult. A million thoughts are flooding my mind, like someone has poured out one hundred marbles on to a concrete floor and I am hustling to catch them all before I lose one.

I run into the bathroom. My hands are shaking so badly I have to grab the doorknob with one hand to steady the other, so I can lock the door. Sweat pours down the sides of my face. I can feel my heart beating in my temples.

Curled up in a ball between the sink and the toilet, I can't move. I want to cry out for help because this feels like the end for me, but I don't. I want this to be the end. I don't want to live through this. I don't want to face any of it.

But, what about them?

I don't respond to the thought, or whatever it is. I ignore it and try to succumb to the darkness. The cold, peaceful, black hole that I have been tiptoeing around for months. I'm right on the edge of it. I want to fall right into that ecstasy of emptiness. Half of my body is hanging right over the edge, but why can't I just fall?

Think about your mom, your sisters, your Grandmother. They need you. Mick needs you.

I see their faces. My mom is sitting in a corner, knees tucked up to her chest, straight faced, tears pouring down. The twins hold on to each other, crying out for mom. Grandma is on her knees, screaming up toward the ceiling. All the cries come together in unison, the loud out cry jolting me back to reality. Suddenly, I am back in the bathroom. Right in front of me, close enough that I can see his ocean blue irises, is Adar.

Jozi.

He gently grabs both of my shoulders and immediately the quaking inside stops. My entire body grows calm.

Jozi…

My breathing slows. I focus my eyes on his, the bright emerald right at the center.

"Adar!" I cry.

He envelopes me with his big arms. He rocks me back and forth. The slow and steady motion soothes me.

Oh, Jozi. God's will, will be done.

"What *is* His will, Adar?"

He's only good, Jozi. He is light and there's no darkness in Him.

Over and over again, I he repeats, *He's only good...He's only good...He's only good.*

He continues to rock me until I drift off into a deep sleep. I dream of floating. I am floating on a big puffy white cloud through a starry night sky, where all the lights of the universe are present. As I float toward the biggest light of them all, I feel lighter—inside and out.

The closer I float toward the light, I feel stronger, instead of hotter, like I could shoot from this position straight through the sky like a rocket. Closer and closer I drift, until I am all encompassed by the light, until my entire body glows as bright as the sun.

30 | Three More Days

It's Friday and Mick is still asleep. I did find out from Grandma, because mom is convinced that I'm too fragile to hear the truth, Mick is in a coma. Yesterday, as I walked into the room while they were removing all of the tubes from his nose and mouth, I thought he was gone.

My heart stopped beating.

Then, I saw Mom's mouth form into a smile. Grandma walked over and whispered the answer to my unspoken questions.

"He's doing better, she said." "He's breathing on his own now, but they say he's still in a coma."

Now, here I sit. Alone with Mick.

"Good morning, Dad." I rub the back of his hand. He's warm, but he still seems lifeless.

"Mom's smile hasn't faded since the moment they took the tube out of your mouth. She even got up with Grandma to get something to eat from the cafeteria. The twins went back to school today. It was their idea.

They are so much more mature in that way. I admire them for that. Sometimes, deep down, I wish I could be more like them.

Well, today is the last day of my suspension and Monday I have to face the consequences of my depression, anxiety, suicide attempts, or whatever everyone knows about me. The truth is, Dad, I tremble at the thought of it. How am I supposed to finish the year like a normal junior with everyone knowing every one of my secrets? Kyell has his girlfriend, so he probably won't have time for pitiful Jozi anymore. How am I supposed to act normal around him now? Tough? Like nothing ever happened?

So much has happened!

Look at you. You are asleep, probably hoping you get to stay in that wonderful dream you are having and here I am talking about all my problems.

I'm sorry, Dad. I'm sorry for all of the trouble I have brought you over the past year. I promise, if you wake up, I won't be this selfish ball of rage I have become. I'm going to spend time with you. I'm going to laugh at every single lame joke you tell me. I will spend quality time with the twins and actually listen to them. When you want to know how my day was, I will give you every boring detail.

I want you to know that you are the best dad I could have ever been given. You are kind, brilliant, a provider, and an amazing artist! Dad, the mural you painted in my room is breath taking! If I had one of those expensive cameras like Kyell, I would take beautiful photos of it and send them to—you know—one of those galleries. Maybe you could get paid to...

"I can let you borrow it, you know."

I turn around, startled. Kyell is standing in the doorway.

"How long have you been there?" I turn back to Mick—wondering how much has he heard of what I said.

"Long enough to hear about the mural Mick painted in your room."

"Oh."

I can feel the warmth of his presence next to me now.

"Why didn't you tell me? I had to find out from people at school."

I turn to look at him, "People at school?"

"Yeah, everyone knows, Jo. It was all over the news. Your dad's a hero."

"Why?" I scowl. Things like this happen all the time on T.V. People get shot everyday over something stupid.

"When that drug dealer got put away a lot of the drug rings where raided. A lot of people were arrested. That guy who shot your dad was just another ring leader who was out to get revenge, but they caught him. He's going to be in jail for a long time. This whole thing has caused a string of arrests. The streets are a lot safer now."

"Yeah, at the expense of my dad's life."

"But, he's getting better. Your mom just said so."

I roll my eyes, unwilling to get my hopes up. And he has some nerve? How can he just pop up and act as if everything between us is okay?

"Look, Jozi, you have to learn to accept the positives that happen in life," he grabs my hand and squeezes gently. "Everything is going to be okay." He turns to face me and softly turns my face toward his. "Mick is going to be okay."

I look up at his warm eyes staring back down at me. He runs his fingers down my cheek and slowly traces it down to my chin. He moves in closer, taking one step toward me. I can hardly breath. Goose bumps cover my body.

"What—are—you doing, Ky?"

He tilts my chin up slowly toward his mouth. I close my eyes, seeing nothing, but replaying this exact image I have imagined 50 times over. Wanting this moment to last forever, I feel his breath on my lips.

Is this really happening today, right now, next to my dad's hospital bed?

Reality sets in. I pull away. "Wait."

He looks at me fiercely. His body is firm and unmovable. "What's wrong?"

"Everything?"

"But,—you love me, right?"

"Yes. I mean? I don't know."

He turns away, running his hand through his hair.

Oh, how I've missed seeing him do that.

"Your dad and I talked. He took me to dinner the day before he got shot, just to hang out. He kind of helped me realize how much I do care for you. I don't know if it's love, but I thought…"

"That kissing me in my dad's hospital room would give you clarity?"

He takes a step toward me, closing the space between us once again, but now he's so close his hair brushes my forehead. "Yes. I've missed you so much, Jo. The days without you, since the day of the fight, have felt like—hell—and like something is missing in my life.

He grabs my hand and brings it up to his lips. He kisses my palm.

My limbs go numb. Once, this was everything I wanted. But now, I don't know how to feel.

I gently remove my hand from his and take a step back.

"Kyell, you are not in love with me. I know this is a lot for you. I understand how close you are to my dad, but don't let all of this mess with your head and your heart."

"What do you mean? I thought this is what you wanted. I thought this is why you have been so angry with me lately.

I see now, Jozi…" His voice trails down to a whisper. "I see you."

"Kyell, I love you. And I cannot tell you how much of a relief it is for you to finally know it. For years I have held this from you, but I never wanted your love to be out of…"

"Out of what?" With a squared jaw, he looks directly through me.

I can't find the right word. My mind goes blank, "I just don't want *this.*"

Kyell runs his hands through his hair again, but this time he leaves them there, "Wait, I'm confused. You love me, but you don't want me to love you back."

"Right. This is forced. You feel sorry for me. We haven't seen each other in a while. You love and respect my dad. You don't want to hurt me. We are best friends. There's so many things that could be causing you to say and do this today."

He lets his arms drop back down with a loud gesture. "Does this sudden change have anything to do with Zeem?"

"No. I just…"

Kyell shoves his hands done in his pockets. He does this when he is frustrated. "Say it Jozi. Just confess it. You are seeing my best friend just to get back at me."

Dumbfounded, I blurt out, "What?"

"Yeah, Chad told me you two have been talking A LOT. You blocked me and Zeem has basically stopped talking to me. What else could be going on."

"You are right, we have talked more than we ever have before, I did block you because you are in love with my ex-best friend and dating her, so what! This is such a double standard; Kyell and you have the nerve to believe your silly friend Chad—of all people? Zeem is my friend. That's it!

He shushes me, putting a figure up to his mouth.

I lower my voice looking out at the empty desk across from my dad's room. "I have the right to be friends with anyone I chose, but you did not have the right to begin dating that…"

"Wow." He stares down at the ground.

"backstabbing, fake, liar."

Moments pass before either of us speak again. I walk back over to Mick's side and sit down. I break the silence.

"What happened?"

He looks over at me with a confused look. "What do you mean?"

"You're here, trying to find an emotional connection with me, what do you think? What happened to you and Shelly."

He exhales. "We broke up."

"Oh. Wow. That was quick. Why?"

He looks at me with eyes that can tear through a brick wall. "Because she's not you."

Kyell walks over to the entrance of the room. "Please text me if anything changes with Mr. Skies."

I respond with, "I will," but I don't think he hears me. He is walking into the elevator when the revelation of what he just said to me sets in.

She's not *me*?

⁕⁂⁕

I spend most of the day in a thick fog. People come in and out of the room, but I never see their faces. Mom tries to give me food, but I tell her I'm not hungry. My thoughts are stuck in time. I keep replaying the touch of Kyell's fingers on my skin. I see his eyes.

Was this real? Did the boy that I have loved for most of my life just try to kiss me and I denied him the opportunity?

All I could think about at the time was Shelly and Zeem. I am not one hundred percent sure Zeem is into me as much as I am into Kyell, but maybe I should at least give him a chance. On the other hand, those thoughts would never have come if Kyell and Shelly hadn't become a couple. I don't know how to decipher the emotions and thoughts zooming through my head, so I banish them all.

I need to focus on my dad and him getting well.

The day moves in slow motion, but finally the sun is setting. Mom walks back in the room after talking to dad's doctor. She looks hopeful. Sitting down next to me, she exhales as though all her prayers were in that single breath. She takes a hold of my hand and squeezes it gently.

"Thank you for being such a rock, Jo. I needed that."

A rock? Surprised at the compliment, I smile. "You're welcome, Mom."

"You know, I think you should go home and get some rest. Grandma will stay with me tonight. Take the car."

"Really?!"

Mom hasn't let me drive since I got my license last year. I asked to borrow the car a week after she found out about the cutting. She said no. I knew it was because she didn't trust my mental stability behind the wheel, so I haven't asked since.

"Yes, I trust you to make it home safely," she tightens her grip of my hand.

My feet are suddenly doing a tap dance on the floor. "Can I make one stop?"

"Sure. Where? Kyell's house?"

"No. Do you remember Zeem?"

A beautiful smile forms on her face, "Yes. I remember the handsome Zeem Crawford." She bats her eyes.

I roll mine. "Mom, it's not what you think. I just need to talk to him about something important. It shouldn't take long, and I will call you when I get home."

"No problem. Go ahead. Tell him I said hello.

I give her a strong squeeze and head out the door.

When I arrive at Zeem's house, the sun is making its final encore. I sit in the car, tapping the steering wheel with my thumbs. Should I have come here?

Zeem and I haven't seen each other in person since the day before the fight with Rowan. Even then, we really didn't see each other. I had no idea he noticed my existence until a few days ago. I have always noticed him—sitting with his face in his books, correcting nonsense whenever appropriate, rubbing his chin whenever he is in deep thought, and his strong stride when he is racing.

He's always been right here in front of me, enjoying my presence, while I ignored his, and fawned over Kyell.

I look out the window at the front door and my palms begin to sweat. I stick the key back in the ignition and start the car. Then, a light on the porch comes on. The door opens. Someone in a red t-shirt with the word WINNING across the chest walks out.

It's Zeem. The silhouette and the slight dip in his step give it away. He walks up to the passenger side and attempts to open the door. I quickly try unlocking the door but fail miserably. I fumble—not once, but twice. On my third attempt I finally press the unlock button instead of the lock button. He grins as he slides into the passenger seat with such calm. We exchange sweet, silent emotions. He wears this bashful smile on his face, while I sheepishly smile back at him then focus on the steering wheel.

"So," he finally says, "it's good to see you."

I laugh, but I am at a loss for words.

Talk, Jo, say something!

I look over at him. His smile has matured over the years. I can't believe I have wasted so much time ignoring this beautiful face. He has magically lost his boyish grin overnight. Now, he wears a perfectly sharp jaw line with facial hair covering his chin.

I shift my eyes back to the steering wheel. My hands and underarms are sweating profusely. Why is that? Why can't sweat begin to form on my feet or my shines, where no one will notice. Why in the most embarrassing places of all? Get it together, Jozi.

"How's your dad? I heard about what happened."

My smile fades immediately.

"He's doing better, but he's still in a coma."

"I'm so sorry, Jo." He leans towards me. "I can't imagine how hard this is."

"Yeah, we're praying he pulls through. The doctors say that talking to him helps, so that's what I do when I'm there. Tomorrow, I think I will read him every story I've ever written." I laugh, trying to cut through the thick air.

"That's so cool. You know? The fact you write and all."

"Yeah, I like to write."

I don't notice that my hands are in my lap until I feel his hand touch mine. "You know maybe you could write about us one day."

My breath catches at the sudden electricity running through me. I look over at him and smile, welcoming his kind touch.

The silence returns and we both just stare out into the night. He slowly pulls his hand back into his lap.

A million thoughts and questions pass through my mind, but I wait. I wait for him to initiate the conversation. I don't want to fumble over my words or say something I will regret.

"So, have you talked to Kyell lately." he finally says.

"Yes." It's all I can manage. I don't know the basis for the question.

"Did he tell you how he feels about you?"

I turn my head to look at him. He gives me a strong stare, one that says *I'm concerned, answer truthfully.*

"Yes. Yes, he did."

"And how did that go?"

"Not so good."

He takes his time responding. He looks down at his hands, then back at me. "What happened?"

"I told him that he's just confused because of everything that's going on. You know the relationship he has with my dad, him and Shelly breaking up, he close relationship with me and everything that's going on with me—it's all just out of confusion. I never wanted him to make his decision based on circumstances but based on how he truly feels."

I gaze out the window realizing just how much I have shared in just one breath. I let all of what I said sink in before I start again.

"Zeem?" I look at him. "Can I ask you something?"

"Anything," he says with absolution.

"Are you…" I pause because I don't know if it's coming out right, "Do you…" I just can't seem to say it.

"Yes," he responds to the unasked question.

"Really?"

"Since the first day of our freshman year. You were walking down the hall with Kyell. He and I had talked about you for the first time that summer. He told me about how close you two were, but I didn't believe that a boy and a girl could be so close and only be friends. You two proved me wrong when I saw you two holding hands. All I could see was your big blond afro—like a golden halo had been placed on your head. You looked like spring and summer all wrapped into one. I wanted to get to know you. I wanted to be your friend."

Zeem glances at me with a slight smile. "When you got a little closer, that was it for me. As far as I was concerned, there was only you and I standing in that hallway that day. You quietly stood there, taking in the stampede, unbothered by the people pushing past you. Your cheeks were flushed, like someone had just pinched them, but the look in your eyes…"

He pauses.

"What look?"

When I found out that you and Kyell really weren't a couple, I was so pumped, but I knew from the start that you were into him. I could see it in your eyes—like you belonged to him. I didn't want to come between something that was, in my mind, bound to happen.

"So, you thought that him and I would eventually…"

"Yeah. But, this year, I decided to do me. If you brushed me off, at least I tried. But, if you were interested, the wait of the past two years would have been worth it."

He sits looking at me, I guess waiting for me to reply, but I don't.

He asks, "So, are you interested?"

"I don't know. I mean—I think you are amazing, and very—attractive." We both grin and blush simultaneously.

He gazes down at his hands to hide it. "But after what happened today—I just don't think that right now is a good time. There's so much I still need to figure out about me—my life."

Zeem reaches out for my hand this time. I willingly place my hand in his.

"I will wait," he says.

Right in the center of my chest, a sense of warmth spreads to every extremity. This unknown feeling surprises me. I never knew those feelings were present for Zeem. Maybe they were tucked away and suffocated by the feelings I have—had—for Kyell, but here and now I realize they are definitely present and real.

"Does Kyell know?"

"How I feel about you? Yeah. I told him. Which is why I think he is all of the sudden acting this way."

He looks out the window at his house. "He was surprised but tried to play it off."

"I see."

"But I don't know. Who knows, maybe he has felt this way the whole time," he shrugs, then looks back at me. "I couldn't sit back anymore, though. It was getting to me." He turns to face me. "I had to let you both know. Now, it's up to you." Zeem turns my face towards his. My cheeks war. "I won't pressure you. If you decide to choose the person who made you their first choice, let me know." He looks deep into my eyes. "Like I said, I will wait."

He leans in and gives me a soft kiss on the cheek. And just like that, I'm smitten.

31 | One More Day

Today, I feel like I'm having one of those dreams again. You know, the ones where you wish you are dreaming because things are going so bad.

Although my suspension was technically up on Friday, the weekend was supposed to be my time to prepare my mind for the stares, the whispers, and laughs that would paint the halls. Instead, I am troubled with other things.

So much has happened, I desperately want to wake up from this dream but there's no blinking my way out of this one. Not even a rapid shake of my head is going to make this all go away.

I let my eyes rest on my now sky-blue ceiling, with small brush-stroked circles that increase in size as my eyes move from the ceiling to the wall. My room makes me feel safe— like I could just fly away for a while to regain some normalcy.

Mom calls out for Hazel and Hannah. My dad is still asleep. Maybe he will wake up today. We all are going to visit him in a little while, so I text Kyell.

Jo: Hey, Ky. My family and I are going to visit dad today. Nothing has changed with his condition

Ky: Ok.

I almost get annoyed that I'm following up with his request, but I brush it off. All this time, I have loved him with my whole heart, and now, I don't know what I feel. I mean, I love him, but the warm sensation I used to feel inside whenever I thought of him isn't there anymore. At this point, my main concern is our friendship. *Will it ever be the same?* I need him right now, but I can't even talk to him.

"Jozi! Are you awake?" My mom yells.

"Yes, ma'am!"

"Okay! We are leaving in an hour!"

"Alright! I will be ready by then."

I exhale loudly into the air. School? Tomorrow? The black hole inside of me feels as though it is enlarging, and I start to panic. My breathing picks up and I search for Dr. Brasser's number. My vision is blurred from tears building up. I can't believe I actually want to talk to her, but I do.

Sitting up quickly, I blink my eyes to clear my vision. Come on, Jozi, not now. I think of my mom. She has so much going on right now. I slide my finger through my contacts. Frustration floods my body. I'm shaking. Once I find the number, before I hit the call button, I hear the familiar sound. The sound that I have grown accustomed to hearing when I'm in some type of trouble.

baa-boom…baa-boom…baa-boom

I sit the phone down next to me. My breathing slows.

"I know you're here."

Yep. I'm here.

"So how long are we going to do this?"

Do what?

"I have an anxiety attack and you show up to make sure no one finds out about it."

He doesn't answer. In my peripheral, I see rapid movements of light. I turn to try to look at him, but my eyes squint at the mirage.

"Adar?"

I'm here.

"Why can't I see you?"

There's no need for you to see me right now. Just know, I am here. I am always here.

⁂

By the time we leave for the hospital, that foggy moment of despair seems like it happened days ago. Dr Brasser may be right about one thing—the mind is fickle.

The twins are quiet in the back seat, as they have been since this all happened. Mom is humming something that I can't quite catch the tune of. Then it hits me, "Aint' No Mountain High Enough." I don't bother joining in. It's just not my thing, but it's good to see her in an upbeat mood.

I gaze out the window, watching the blur of color soaring by. Once we get to the hospital it's difficult to find parking. We circle the lot several times before mom decides to try to find parking in the parking garage. She fusses the entire half mile to the spinning door entrance. The hospital is super busy today. Sundays always are.

"Why is the hospital always so busy on Sunday?" I ask.

We walk to the elevator. Hannah and Hazel race each other to press the button. Hazel gets there first. Hannah groans.

"Well, it is the weekend and most people think visiting on Sunday after church is the right thing to do." Mom replies.

"And how do you know this?" I roll my eyes.

"Just look around..." She gestures for me to look. I notice that most of the people coming in are dressed to the nines. "Do you see what I see?"

"Yes, but I think it's just a coincidence. Maybe a lot of people got sick this weekend."

She waves my suggestion away. "Whatever, Jozi."

The elevator dings, and from a distance I hear my name called. I turn to look in the direction of the voice. Running toward me is a slender girl with a thick brown bob. I try to make out who it is, but the name just isn't registering.

"Who is that, Jo?" my mom asks.

"I'm not quite sure. Go on without me. I will be up soon."

The elevator door shuts. I start to walk toward this person and realize who it is.

"Shelly? You cut your hair?"

"Yeah." She's panting and runs her fingers through her hair nervously, "It was time for a change."

I don't know what to say. Part of me feels a little angry with her for cutting off her beautiful hair, and another part of me feels triumphant because there's just one less thing to make her, "Miss. Perfect." She looks average now—like we could be on an even playing field. Maybe.

I push those thoughts away—all the way to the back of my mind. *Be nice, Jozi.*

"It looks—great! Then again, your hair before was amazing. Why did you cut it?"

"I told you." she fidgets with her purse. "It was time for a change."

We both look down at the floor, as if we will find in the tile the next words that should come out of our mouths. She speaks first.

"How's your dad?"

"Not so good, but he's doing better. He's—still asleep."

"Asleep?"

"Yeah. That's what I like to call it, a deep sleep. It sounds better than saying he's in a coma."

"You're right—it does."

The elevator has dinged at least twice. I want to join my family, but I stay. I wonder if she's here to see someone.

"Were you coming up?"

"Well, I'm kinda glad I caught you down here. I hate hospitals, but I had to talk to you. I just—I just wanted to see if you were okay. You know—a lot has happened since the last time we saw each other." She shifts, and adjusts her purse on her shoulder, "A lot has happened in the past *year*."

We make eye contact for the first time and I can see the sincerity that was once there years ago.

"I know."

"Can we sit down for a minute? I promise I won't keep you long."

"Sure." Although she is the main reason I am suspended, she has this hold on people that just causes you to be nice to her.

We head over to the lobby that makes up the center of the hospital. It seems more crowded than before, but no one is occupying this space. Everyone is trying to get to their loved ones in a hurry and has no time for sitting. I wonder why the lobby is here in the first place, but instead of hurrying to my loved one, I take a seat on one of the large gray leather couches with the girl who betrayed me.

I don't know what to expect from this conversation. Shelly has been full of surprises since she started making other friends. My mind is telling me to shut her down—to make her feel as horrible as she has made me. My heart is telling me to hear her out—to give her another chance. Then again, I don't know why she's here. She says she wanted to see if I am okay, but what does that mean? I have a lot going on, so that can mean so many things.

Am I okay with her telling my secret? Am I okay with her dating Kyell? Am I okay with her not having my back? Or am I okay that my dad is in a deep sleep and may not wake up?

Just thinking about it makes my heartbeat speed up.

"What's up, Shelly? I really need to get upstairs with my family."

"Okay, I will make this quick. I'm sure you know about Kyell and me, but that's not what I am here for."

"Yes. I know and I'm okay with that."

"Good, because I really like him, Jo. We are not doing so good right now, but I'm sure we will get over it." She looks unsure, which brings me a small dose of gratification.

I roll my eyes. "If you are not here about that, what is it?"

"It's about Rowan."

"Really. You came all the way here to talk to me about the girl who practically ruined my life?"

I get up to leave, but Shelly grabs my arm.

"Wait, please listen to what I have to say. It's up to you what you do with it, but I thought it was important for me to make a mends here—since it is partly my fault all this happened in the first place."

"Partly. How about one-hundred percent your fault."

"Wait a minute, Jozi, you could have just gotten up out of that desk and no one would know about…"

"That was never your business to tell, Shelly!"

She hangs her head. "I know. I know I was wrong. I am truly sorry for that, Jo. I was just trying to help…"

"Come on, spit it out, Shelly? I really need to get going."

"Okay, you know how you had some secrets you didn't want anyone to know?"

"Yes."

"Well, Rowan has some secrets of her own…"

"And I don't care to know any of them."

"I wasn't going to tell you. I just wanted you to know that you and Rowan have a lot in common. She may be a bully now, but you remember how sweet she was just a year ago. She is going through a tough time and—I just wanted you to take that into consideration. You come back tomorrow…"

"Don't' remind me."

"I don't want you to see her and think of her as your enemy. We need each other."

"I can't make you any promises, Shelly. In my mind she couldn't have done anything more awful than what she did. I don't think I could ever forgive what she did."

"I would say to put yourself in her shoes, but you are practically already in them. She is going through some of the same things you are going through, but a whole lot worse, Jozi. Have you ever stopped to think why I would tell her your secret? It wasn't to shame you. It was to show her someone who was hanging on. Someone strong."

Shelly rises to her feet and from a far I hear my mom calling out for me. I turn to look for her. She is running towards me, yelling something I can't make out. Leaving Shelly behind, I run towards her.

"He's awake!" She yelps.

Without a second thought, I rush to the elevator with mom. When the elevator dings and the doors shut, I can barely breath.

"So—how? What happened?"

Also trying to catch her breath, she says, "Hazel and Hannah started singing our song—you know the one Mick and I danced to when…"

"Yeah—yeah. The one you have been humming all day."

"Yeah! That one. You know it's strange—I woke up with that in my head this morning."

"Okay, mom. What happened?"

The elevator stops on floor five. An elderly couple slowly get on.

"So, the twins started singing, "Ain't No Mountain High Enough," and all of the sudden Mick started to hum along. They were so shocked that they stopped singing, so I motioned for them to continue. After the first verse, he tried to sing the first word of the chorus. When he did his started to cough. Violently. Hazel pressed the call button for the nurse and that's when I came to get you."

The elevator finally reaches the 12th floor. As politely as we can, we push pass the elderly couple. As we rush down the hall, my mind goes down a dark path and I begin to think the worst.

He's gone. I'm too late. Shelly ruins everything.

Mom rushes into the room full of doctors. From the door way I can see that they all acknowledge her, but their faces are unreadable. I can't tell if they are telling her he's dying or if he will be going home tomorrow.

In that moment, I feel a set of arms wrap around my waist. Then another set. The twins are holding on to me like Dad's life depends on their grip, so I hold on to them as if we are his lifeline.

32 | Never the Same

When mom finally comes out, her face is emotionless. The twins release me and quickly run to her. My breath comes back in gasps. I try to read her—her body language, eyes, but nothing. The twins are drowning her with questions, not giving her enough time to respond. She fixes her eyes on mine and slowly walks toward me. My eyes fill with tears.

"What—what's wrong?"

Her lips curl into a smile, "Nothing's wrong." She throws her arms around me, "For once, nothing's wrong."

I release my breath, collapsing to the floor. The twins giggle in relief. There in the middle of the hallway, we all cry and laugh simultaneously. People walking by stare, but we ignore them. Nothing can disturb our happiness.

After I gather myself off the floor. Mom insists that we talk before I head into the room.

"Your dad is going to be a little different for a while, Girls."

I continue to smile through the news.

"The trauma to his brain has caused blurred vision and slurred speech. He will also be wheelchair bound for the next six to nine months. It all depends on how quickly his brain heals." My body tenses, but I try to remain calm. She goes on.

"But, there's some good news." She lights up when she tells us. "The good news is with therapy and time, he will recover."

I take it all in with one big breath, then I let it out slowly. We look at each other for strength. Things won't be the same for a while, but he will recover and there's hope. That's more than I could wish for.

Mom pulls us all in for a hug. "You girls have to wait in the lobby for a little while. The doctors want to run more tests and allow your dad some time to get used to being awake again."

I settle in to a corner near the window. I stare down at the pedestrians coming and going for what seems like hours. At some point, I guess I fall asleep because I am jolted awake with Hannah, yelling, "We can go see him now!"

The twins beat me there by at least thirty seconds. They are occupying both sides of the bed when I walk through the door. Dad is sitting up with a few new cords trailing from his nostrils and chest. His head is still wrapped in the bandages, but I can tell they are fresh. He's grown a beard in the past few days, which makes him look older. He turns his head slightly when I walk into the room.

"Jo," he says and reaches out one hand.

I walk toward him slowly. Tears begin to form behind my eyes, and I try to hold them at bay. The sensation is so painful it burns, then I realize there's no controlling what's about to happen. Before I reach the bed side my cheeks are wet. Mick attempts to pull me in, grunting in the process.

"Careful, Dad," I say.

I sit down on the edge of the bed and lean in gently. I lightly lay my head on his chest, grateful for the sound of his heartbeat. The twins and mom close in around us. Everyone begins to cry. As the tears flow heavily down my face, I feel brand new. My family had always seemed like an obstacle to my happiness. In my eyes, they were one of the main reasons my life was so difficult. Maybe they are all crying in relief, but for me the tears are for something else.

I lay there, holding on to my fragile dad—the only dad I have ever known—knowing that the way I see *life* will never be the same.

33 | Back to School

If I have ever said that The Man in the Sky doesn't exist, maybe it's because I never experienced anything like what I have been experiencing the past two weeks. Yesterday definitely gave me even more hope that there just might be a higher power working in my favor.

I feel different—like I can face anything—I mean, at least I got up when the alarm went off. Now, I'm hiding out in the bathroom with both doors locked, hoping mom will forget that I'm even in here. She took the day off because she has to take me to school and sign me back in.

I was confused why she wanted to take the entire day off for something that will take only five to ten minutes. I was perplexed. This is not like her. But there's good reason, she wants to spend the day with dad.

I lean over the sink, staring myself right in the eyes. *Wow.* I get a little closer. My eyes…they are—beautiful. They are a shade darker than my hair, but this morning they are glowing like auburn light bulbs. I smile at myself and toss my loose curls from one side to the other.

Then, I remember the inevitable.

"Adar, if there ever was a day I needed a pep talk, this is the day."

I look around.

Nothing.

I listen carefully for the now familiar thud of that blue ball.

Nothing.

I give it a try.

Okay, Jozi. There's nothing to be nervous about. Teens are just people too. I'll just stare right back at them and keep it moving. The look I give them will make them remember what I did to Rowan, and they won't dare whisper about me or look in my direction again.

Now. Now. Is that the right way to think?

"Adar!" I do a full 360, looking for any sign of him.

I told you, I am always here. You don't have to see me or hear me for that to be true.

"It doesn't matter. I'm just happy you are here."

I want you to do something for me, Jozi.?

"I guess, but can you make time speed up like, maybe a week, so I don't have to experience this week? I mean, you took me back in time, can't you move me forward in time?"

Sorry. No can do my friend.

"Wow, Adar. Some guardian you are."

Now, look at yourself in the mirror.

I groan in protest. "Sure. Why not. I've been admiring my eyes today. Did you do something to them. I've never noticed how pretty they are."

I stare back at myself, admiring what I see, I smile again. Adar ignores me and continues.

Say to yourself these words: I am strong.

"I am strong."

He then says, *I am beautiful,* and I follow suit. By the end, I made four declarations that set off a fire in me, hot enough to push me to get dressed. I decide on wearing an orange v-neck shirt, a pair of jeans, and some gold baby doll flats. Mick once told me orange is my color, so I decide to wear orange in honor of him. I run down stairs just as mom is heading up the stairs.

"Oh," she says, "I was just coming up there to get you.

"No need. I'm ready."

She looks at me with questions in her eyes, but she smiles and says, "Okay, let's go."

When we get to the school, the first period bell is just ringing. Everyone who's late is now running in, trying to make sure they don't get that green slip. Mom parks the car, turns off the engine, and just sits there. I don't move because I can sense the proverbial pep talk is just seconds away.

"Jozi?"

"Yes, Mom?"

"You know you don't have to do this. I've been looking up some good online courses for high schoolers."

"Oh, now you tell me." I throw my hands up in the air dramatically.

She looks at me with sad eyes. "I'm sorry, honey. I just thought…"

"It's okay, Mom. I'm kidding. One thing I would hate more than coming back to this place is being alone. I really don't want that."

"Right—," She turns toward me with excitement in her voice, "Because you do have friends—like Kyell, and Zeem." Her voice trails down playfully, as she mentions Zeem's name.

"Stop it, Mom." I roll my eyes.

"I think you are making the right decision, Jo. You can do this. And if for some reason you change your mind, just let me know."

"Okay."

She grabs a hold of my hand. "Immediately."

"I will."

Walking through those double doors doesn't playout the same way it did in my imagination nor my nightmares. I imagined everyone lining the hallways, waiting for me—whispering and pointing at me. Instead, the hallways are practically empty.

We sit in the office for about five minutes, then Mr. Donovan walks in with one of those fake, "I'm happy to serve you," smiles.

"Mrs. Skies—Miss Skies, come on back."

He holds the half-wooden door for us, as we walk through. Mr. Donovan's office is without a doubt one of my favorite places in the entire school, apart from the library. I don't get to see it much—and the last time I was in here, I couldn't care less—but the ambiance is breathtaking. There are books everywhere!

We sit down in the comfy, burgundy chairs and he takes his seat behind his desk. He weaves his hands together in front of him and shows off his pearly whites. Mr. Donovan would be a handsome man if he had hair.

"So, Miss. Skies, are you ready?"

"As ready as I will ever be," I reply.

He clears his throat. "I just want to reassure both of you that the administrative team has done everything in their power to ensure that you are coming back to a safe zone. If anything occurs that you are uncomfortable with, please let me or your counselor, Ms. Baker, know."

I nod my head. "Yes, Sir."

After signing me in, Mom gives me a big hug and I head to my first period class. By the time I get to the second floor, my reserve gives way to sweaty arm pits and heavy breathing.

I do a bee line to the bathroom instead of going to class. When I go to push the door open, a flood of memories from two weeks ago stops me in my tracks. I push through the memory and the door.

Right next to the sink, I throw my bookbag down. I turn on the faucet to throw some cold water on my face, take three deep breaths in, and slowly let them out. Looking up at myself in the mirror, I begin to say the declaration Adar lead me through this morning, in hopes that it would give me the surge I need once again.

You are strong. You are beautiful. You are enough. There's no one like you. Then, I hear a toilet flush. Embarrassment quickly covers my face. Why didn't I check the stalls? I pat my face dry quickly praying whoever this is didn't hear me. Out walks Rowan Backskill.

She looks dumbfounded for a moment. "Oh—hey," she says dully.

Be nice, Jozi. Be nice.

"Hey."

She walks past me to the sink right next to mine. I grab my bag, checking my hair one more time before I leave.

"Hey, Jozi?"

Weirded out that she would even speak to me a second time, I answer reluctantly, "Yeah?"

"What were you saying to yourself. You know, before I walked out?"

"Oh. Um…"

She looks at me. Hair just as perfect as it's always been—thick, red, wavy. Her eyes look a little strained, but I try not to keep eye contact for too long.

"I—t's just something I say to—you know—encourage myself."

"Oh. I see." She looks at herself in the mirror.

There's a long pause and I take that as the cue to leave, but before I can grab my bag, she gently hands it to me.

"I know I said some horrible—horrible things to you, but..." she hangs her head, "There's no excuse. I'm sorry, Jozi. God's knows I had no right and I was wrong. So wrong."

Her eyes are intense—sincere even. Looking into her eyes I also detect regret. She's just as broken as I was a few weeks ago.

Like a vapor, I feel my anger towards her disappear.

"Thanks, Rowan. I'm sorry, too."

She releases the strap of my bookbag and turns to look at herself in the mirror once again. "Thanks, Jozi."

"No problem."

Before I can reach the door, she asks, "So, can you tell me what to say?" She wipes a few tears from her eyes. "I need a bit of encouragement today, too."

"Um—Okay. It's just four declarations about who you are."

I put down my bookbag and face the mirror with her. Our reflections, side by side.

"Repeat after me: *You are strong. You are beautiful. You are enough. There is no one like you.*"

When we are finished, surprisingly, she reaches out for a hug. It's awkward, but I don't shut her down. We both walk out the bathroom ready for the harsh reality high school will reveal to us today. She walks in one direction and I in the other. Who would have known I would be the one encouraging Rowan, or anyone, two weeks ago?

Maybe broken people aren't unfixable. I should know.

34 | A New Chapter

Several Weeks later

Today is the last day of school, and I am so ready for the lazy walks at Alki Beach, never ending weekends, and filling up my journals with story after story. Usually, getting out of bed is a chore, but today I feel so eager to get to school. As I jump out of bed, a knock comes to my door.

"Come in!"

Hannah sticks her head in, "Can I borrow your black flats?"

"Sure."

The twins are less annoying, but they haven't fully loss their ability to make me exit a room. Since Mick came home a few weekends ago, they have been extra clingy. I don't blame them though, things are different around here, and I could use some normalcy too. Being their normal is weird, but a real confidence boost. I guess my nasty attitude does have its upside.

Mom hasn't been working as much because she has to do a lot more around the house. She seems happier than I have ever seen her, though. The other day she actually got home early and cooked! She made my favorite, crab cakes and cheesy grits. There wasn't any left for seconds. I told her she needs to come home earlier more often. Mick laughed and made a joke about the Hamburger Helper he made the night before that no one even finished.

Mick is still in a wheelchair, but he tries to make himself useful. He came out and told the twins and I he wouldn't be returning to the firm. We all got a little worried. I guess he could see the evidence on our faces, so he immediately told us the rest of the plan. It turns out that Mick has always wanted to be a graphic designer and took some courses for it a few years after he finished his law degree. He told us his plan to finish the degree and to open his own business.

It didn't surprise me. The man has an artistic eye.

Mom chimed in to assure us that we are okay financially, and that she supports Mick wanting to take this time to start something new.

"And online school kind of works—since I'm stuck in this mobile desk." Mick said.

Silence.

I looked at him, he looked at me, then at the twins. Then—it hit me. That was supposed to be funny. So, I laugh out loud—to appease him.

"Ha ha ha. Wow! That was funny."

They all looked at me then cleared the room. Some things always stay the same, I guess.

So, my family life has been different—but good. There's absolutely nothing I care to complain about.

Life at Clearview High has been odd though. Not the kind of odd I experienced before my encounter with Rowan, but even more odd. When I came back to school, it seemed that no one even noticed I was gone.

No one mentioned the fight. No one mentioned the depression. Everyone acted like the whole event never happened. To make it even odder, everything has been cool with Rowan and I since that day in the bathroom.

Sometimes, when she does come to school, she sits with me during lunch. She doesn't say much, but I'm okay with that. Her and Shelly don't seem as close any more and I'm not sure if it's because Shelly has a boyfriend now, or what. Kyell and Shelly got back together a few weeks after I came back. I wasn't sure if he fixed things between them because he wanted to hurt me or if it was the stalker-ish way Shelly always appeared whenever we were out together. She really worked hard to get his attention.

Kyell eventually came to his senses about us. He stopped being mad at me for turning him down. I really think he was mad because it hurt his pride more than the fact that he was madly and deeply in love with me.

Our friendship is different now, but that's okay. I understand why. Sometimes when you cross the line of friendship, things can get all tangled up, like one of those chain necklaces. It takes a lot of care and attention to untangled, if that is even possible.

We both are looking forward to our senior year. The year where everything is supposed to fall into place. I don't know about him, but I feel like everything has already fallen into place. My parents both agreed to let me major in journalism instead of medicine. I don't know what came over them, but I'm willing to bet that Grandma Ellis had something to do with it. If that's the case, I am so grateful. I can just see myself walking the streets of New York, headed to my corner office, with a window, as the editor and chief of some major publishing company and maybe authoring some books of my own, or even a juicy column—I don't know. I just feel like there's so many possibilities now.

I run downstairs after getting dressed. The twins have already left and I'm thirty minutes early. Mick is sitting at the table having his first of three rounds of coffee and reading one of his text's books on ancient Roman cathedrals. Now, he has to wear reading glasses, but I told him they make him look younger. He didn't buy it, but ironically, it's true.

"Good morning, Dad."

"Good morning, Jo. Are you driving to school today?".

"Maybe."

He cuts his eyes at me, laughing as he continues skimming his book.

"What are you doing today?"

"Well, I think I'm going to finish my 2,000-word paper, that's due at midnight, which I haven't started on—and—finish that painting I started—if I have time."

"Cool…"

From the drive-way, a horn beeps. I make eye contact with Mick and he gives me an all-knowing smile.

"Have a good day, sweetheart."

"I will!"

I bound out the door towards Zeem's, black Challenger. The engine roars as I pull the passenger door open. I blush, at his consistently clever way of acknowledging me.

"Good morning, Beautiful."

"Hi, Babe," I smile back.

As we ride down this street, for the last time as eleventh graders, I am grateful for how different my life is today compared to a few months ago. I lean back in the seat, taking it all in; my new way of seeing life and the people in it, my dream career, friends, summer and this handsome companion sitting next to me.

Suddenly, I feel a slight nudge in my bag.

Zeem notices my alarm. "What's wrong?"

"I—I don't know."

I dig down in my bag searching for the culprit for the small nudge. Shoving my hand down to the very bottom, I feel around until my hand wraps around the object. My breath catches. Slowly, I bring my hand up and out of the bag—shocked at what I find.

"What's—oh. A ball." He laughs.

"Yes. It's a ball."

I smile at the gesture. A small memento left by an amazing friend, who came just when I needed him most. I haven't heard from Adar since my first day back to school. On the days I feel like I need a visit from him, I remember what he said about always being near. At this moment, I feel his presence, so I speak those two enduring words of gratitude…

Thank you.

I am strong. I am beautiful. I am enough.
And there is no one like me.

www.ingramcontent.com/pod-product-compliance
Lightning Source LLC
Chambersburg PA
CBHW051047050726
47592CB00002B/431